Is Everyone **Moonburned** but Me?

Is Everyone Moonburned but Me?

by Stella Pevsner

Clarion Books • New York

Clarion Books
a Houghton Mifflin Company imprint
215 Park Avenue South, New York, NY 10003
Copyright © 2000 by Stella Pevsner

The type for this book was set in 14-point Weiss.
All rights reserved.

For information about permission to reproduce selections
from this book, write to Permissions, Houghton Mifflin Company,
215 Park Avenue South, New York, NY 10003

Printed in the U.S.A.

Library of Congress Cataloging-in-Publication Data

Pevsner, Stella.
Is everyone moonburned but me? / by Stella Pevsner.
p.   cm.
Summary: Thirteen-year-old Hannah feels plain and drab compared to her older and
younger sisters, but when both of her divorced parents seem on the verge of remarriage
and a series of crises face the family, she is the only one who manages to keep her sanity.
ISBN 0-395-95770-2
[1. Self-acceptance Fiction. 2. Family life Fiction. 3. Sisters Fiction. 4. Schools Fiction.
5. Remarriage Fiction.] I. Title.
PZ7.P44815Is   2000
[Fic]—dc21   99-36816
CIP
HAD   10 9 8 7 6 5 4 3 2 1

With special love for Spencer . . .
a most agreeable boy and a born book lover

one

Mom once said, "I can read blueprints, but I can't read my own daughters."

She should have asked me. I could have read my two sisters and myself for her.

My older sister, Melody, Miss Queen Fifteen, is pretty, a smart-mouth, and totally self-involved. Anyone could read her, so where's the mystery? As a house, Melody would have stairs leading nowhere, rooms lined with mirrors, and vents everywhere to get rid of her steam.

Paige, eight, is cute and delicate—and knows how to play both to the max. Her personal blueprint may be still developing, but it packs punch and power. As a house, she would be charming, have lots of little alcoves, and contain a state-of-the-art air purification system to keep her allergies in check.

As Hannah, thirteen, I am neither plain nor pretty, am dependable ("Hannah will do it!"), am always on the honor roll ("But it's so easy for Hannah!"), and am always there to pick up the pieces. I am the most ordinary child in this family. My blueprint would be standard, no surprises. Everything according to plan.

But blueprints can be altered, can't they?

Recently I'd asked this of Dad, just to see what he'd say. He's a builder and deals with house plans all the time. Before he and Mom were divorced, she worked as his business manager. Now she works for a trucking firm, keeping track of drivers, loads, and timetables on her home computer.

"Of course," Dad said in answer to my question. "You surely know, Hannah, that blueprints can be changed in little ways. You have to stick to the basic plan, but you can certainly shift closets and stairways around, even enlarge rooms or make alterations if the client wants to use the space for a different purpose. Why are you asking me this now?" We were at his current building site and I could see I was interrupting.

"But," I persisted, "can you change the way a house is headed?"

"Well, sport, if you're asking can I change a colonial into a modern, the answer is no." He now gave me his full attention. "What are you getting at, anyway?"

"Nothing, really," I said. "I was wondering, I guess, if people can change their basic blueprint. You know, the way they are?"

He frowned slightly. "Is this about your mother and me?"

"Get real, Dad. I know you guys are too old to change."

He laughed. "Thanks for that upbeat comment." Responding to a shout from one of the plumbers, he turned around and called out, "Be right there, Mac." He looked back to me. "Hannah, what's this really all about?"

If I'd said "Nothing," he'd have known I was faking, so I gave him an answer just to put him off. "I was thinking about my friends. Cheyenne's so featherheaded and Kelsey's so dogmatic." (That was a new word I was happy to be able to use.) "I wonder if they'll always be like that."

"Who knows." My friends and their foibles were clearly of no interest to my father. "Got to go, sport. Good of you to stop by. You know I'm always glad to see you."

"Same here. See you Friday night." I got on my bike and pedaled back home.

I guess I've always known where I stand in my family. Right in the middle. Not the adorable firstborn. (Three photo albums of Melody before she got out of Pampers testify to that adorableness.) Since the perfect girl-child couldn't be duplicated, my guess is that they hoped the next one would be a boy. Only I wasn't. Bad move. Then when Paige came along, the fact that here was still another girl was overlooked by the worry of her being so tiny, precious, and delicate.

Even as a little kid, I sensed my position in the family. I knew that Mom's first concern, coming back home from somewhere, was how the girls had managed. Had Paige wheezed or turned blue? Had Melody gotten into Mom's makeup or cut pictures of half-naked people out of *National Geographic*? As for Hannah, she was always okay. She might even have emptied the dishwasher or cleaned the TV screen, which always attracted dust.

Basically I just accepted my role, the way little kids do, without questioning. But lately I've been wondering if that's the way it has to be.

What started my thinking was a day a week or so ago when I was over at Cheyenne's. She and Kelsey and I had pretty much wrapped up nothing-new gab about school almost starting, what classes we'd be in together, and so on. Both Cheyenne's and Kelsey's families had extended trips still to come, but to boring places like state parks. What to do now?

"I know!" Cheyenne said in her animated way. "Let's play What If? It's raining, so we can't go to the mall."

Kelsey rolled her eyes. "Ditz-girl, the stores are all *inside* the mall. So it doesn't matter if it's raining."

"Oh, right," Cheyenne said cheerfully. "But we don't have a ride, so I'll get out the game." She dumped her cat, Mouser, off her lap, ignored his outraged yowls, and got the game book from the shelf. Mouser returned to her side and stared balefully at Kelsey and me, as though we were responsible for his being dumped.

"Oh, hey, guys," Cheyenne said, holding the book, "you know that kid Rick? Rhymes with rich?"

"It doesn't rhyme," Kelsey pointed out.

"Oh, okay. Anyway, he's rich, or at least his folks are. So rich that even his shadow is in color instead of black-and-white."

"So?" I asked, ignoring her little whimsy.

"I saw him yesterday at the Gap. And he said, 'How's it going?'"

When we looked at her blankly, she said, "It's the first time he's ever noticed me. So isn't that significant?"

"Let's play the game," Kelsey said. "Sometime before school starts."

Cheyenne turned a few pages. "Here's a good one: If you could live in luxury anyplace in the world but could never come back to the USA, would you do it? I would, but only if my brothers had to stay here. I'd take Mouser, though."

"Then you'd have to go to a country that allows pets to immigrate," Kelsey said. "Me, I wouldn't go. How about you, Hannah?"

"I'd like to travel, but not for keeps."

"So your answer is no," Kelsey said. "Next question, Cheyenne."

"Okay: If you were in a boat with your mother and the rest of your family and it capsized and she could save just one of you, who would it be? In my family it would be Mouser. Mom loves this cat." Seeing our disgusted looks, she went on. "Okay. Person. Me, I guess. I'm the only girl."

"Are you the favorite kid?" Kelsey asked.

Surprised, Cheyenne said, "Why wouldn't I be?"

"Huh." Kelsey turned to me. "Hannah?"

"You go first," I said. I found the question disturbing.

Kelsey thought a moment. "I guess me. My thinking is, Mom could always get another baby, but not another me. Go, Hannah."

"Well . . . my sister Melody wouldn't go out on a boat unless there was a guy along. So he could save her."

"What about Paige?" Kelsey asked.

I didn't really want to do this. "Paige is delicate, and so Mom would probably save her."

"And leave you to drown?"

"I can swim."

"That's not the point of the question," Kelsey said.

"Yeah," Cheyenne agreed. "Like what if you got knocked out when the boat capsized?"

"She'd still save Paige." I felt a little queasy, as if I really were in a boat.

"Is Paige your mom's favorite?" Cheyenne had stopped petting the cat.

I was thinking it was a toss-up between Paige and Melody, but I said, "It's not a question of favorite, it's . . ." I didn't know how to go on.

"Let's move to the next question," Kelsey said.

Cheyenne read, "If there was a fire in your house and you could save only one possession, what would it be?"

"The locket Grandma Orrington gave me," I said, glad that the question was so easy. I hardly listened as Kelsey said she'd save her antique teddy bear that would grow in value each year and Cheyenne dithered on about her many treasures.

The previous question remained a windstorm in my mind. I'd always known, as I mentioned, that Melody was the ruling princess in our family. All she lacked was the tiara. But she'd been such a pain lately, Mom might welcome the opportunity to give her a boost overboard.

It seemed to me that Paige had moved up to current reigning favorite in Mom's eyes. Of course, my status as middle child remained unchanged. Mom's only reason for saving me would be that she'd come to count on my help around the house.

Now, with Dad it might be a different story. I would never say I'm his favorite—Dad is very fair. But he and I have always been very close. It seemed sometimes that I'd become the boy figure in his life. I was the only one in the family who took an interest in his work.

"Look, it's stopped raining!" Cheyenne said. "Let's walk down to the park and see if the guys are there shooting baskets."

We did, but they weren't. After a while we all went home.

Mom had prepared her usual Sunday dinner, a contrast to the tossed-together weekday meals. "Do you like the mashed potatoes?" she asked. "I put in a little garlic this time for seasoning."

"Garlic," Melody muttered. "Thanks a lot. I have a date tonight with Keith."

"So don't give him the usual four-star kiss like you told me about," Paige said.

"What's this?" Mom asked, on red alert.

"They're good," I broke in. "The potatoes, I mean. But a little watery."

"Thanks so much for the rave comments, girls," Mom said. "All I do is try. For your information, miss," she said to me, "I deliberately used water instead of milk this time, in case the milk was affecting Paige's dairy product allergy."

"How come fun-loving Steve isn't with us tonight?" Melody said. Steve is Mom's boyfriend— or manfriend, I guess you'd say. "Off to the demolition derby?"

"Derby? What are you talking about? He had to go to his parents' house."

"Isn't it about time he took you home to meet his folks?" Melody asked with an innocence that fooled no one.

"I've met his family, missy," Mom said. "Now, could we just be quiet and enjoy our dinner? Unless you have more constructive comments about my cooking?"

"The food's yummy," Paige the suck-up said. "You're a master chef, Mom."

"Thank you, dear." Mom got up to answer the phone. It was Steve, wanting to stop by. That put Mom in a mellow mood, and the meal took an upturn.

Steve arrived soon after we'd finished eating. He's a big guy with a big smile, and would've made a great host on a kids' TV show. Except that his smile was genuine. As always, he greeted us with "Hi, there, kiddos." Melody had mentioned to Mom that when Steve said that, it made her teeth ache, but Mom's only reply was, "Then go see a dentist."

Before they took off, Mom, in her command mode, said, "Girls, take your baths and don't stay up all night."

Melody, who took no orders, left shortly after

that. "She calls Keith her stud-muffin," Paige informed me. "I don't get it."

"There's nothing to get," I said. "Go take your bath."

"In a while," Paige said, turning on the TV.

I went upstairs and picked up a book I'd half-way finished. Except for the faint sound from downstairs of a program my sister probably wouldn't be watching if Mom were home, the house was quiet.

I wondered if I'd ever get used to the split-up of our family. We used to do things together, but now everyone went in different directions.

We three girls used to spend from Friday night until Sunday afternoon with Dad, but now it was a hit-or-miss thing. Melody would rather hang with her friends (mainly Keith) than be with us and Dad. Paige often whined that she didn't feel well and shouldn't be doing the things Dad had planned. I guess Dad got discouraged trying to please everyone.

But didn't he know that I loved spending time with him? That I always enjoyed the outings he set up? In fact, thinking about him just now gave me a great idea. I could go live with Dad. We got along, I didn't give him grief, and as for Mom and the others, what did they care? They were all so wrapped up in themselves they wouldn't even miss me, except for when they wanted me to do something.

I don't know why I'd never thought of this before, but now that I had, it seemed such an obvious thing to do. I wanted to pick up the phone and break the news at once. I'd wait, though, and tell Dad in person and see his look of joy. I smiled, thinking about how great it would be to live with the only person in the family who really valued my company.

two

By Thursday, with both Cheyenne and Kelsey off on their trips, I was totally bored. Paige was at her friend Tamara's house and Mom was, as usual, huddled over the computer.

I went to the doorway of her study. "I think I'll bike over to Dad's construction site," I said. "It's not too far."

"Go ahead." Mom frowned at the screen. "There's a screwup somewhere," she said. "Both of those trucks shouldn't be heading toward the same town." She reached for the phone. "Pick up a carton of milk on your way home," she said, dialing.

Just what I loved to do.

I really enjoyed going to visit whatever building site Dad was working on at the time. I'd see the rough beginning and then watch it develop into an actual place where people would live. Right now Dad was involved in building a whole series of houses in a new development.

I've always loved the smell of new lumber. When I was small and Dad did a carpentry job in our basement, I'd hang around. Sometimes I'd pick up wood shavings and stick them in my hair with bobby pins. "See my curls, Daddy?" I'd say. He'd smile and tell me I was a regular Shirley Temple.

The sawdust heaps on the floor were like beach sand to me. I don't remember this, but Mom says when I was really little, I thought people were stuffed with sawdust like the china antique doll that belonged to my grandmother. One day, when my stomach hurt, I told Mom I had a pain in my sawdust. Mom repeated this to her friends for months, but gave it up when I finally appealed to Dad to make her stop.

When I was about seven, I actually helped Dad build a playhouse for us in the back yard. It was just one room, but with a little attached porch. We painted it white with blue trim around the doors and windows. I think Dad was a little disappointed that I didn't play in it much, but to me the best part had been building it.

Melody didn't find a use for it either, until she

was about thirteen. One day Mom saw smoke coming out of the playhouse and in a panic called the fire department. All they found was Melody, stomping out papers that had ignited from her cigarette. She was terrified, and Mom was furious. "If this happens again, young lady," she said, "you won't need a fire truck but an ambulance!"

That's typical of Mom—empty threats—but as far as I know Melody never smoked again. At least not around the house.

It was Paige who finally made use of the playhouse. She's out there a lot, playing dolls with her friends.

Now, with Dad out of the house and most of his tools and equipment gone as well, I don't have a chance to help build things anymore. I suppose he could find odd jobs for me at the building site, but it would be against union rules, as well as an insurance problem.

When I finally reached the construction site, I saw Dad's car but not him. I went over to where his long-time carpenter, Sam, was cutting a piece of lumber with an electric saw. When he'd finished and noticed me, he smiled. "Hey, Hannah," he said. "Come to check out the progress?"

"Yeah," I said. "I hear you guys need some expert advice."

"That's about it." He looked at the two-by-four. "So tell me, have you decided to be a builder when you grow up? Or are you going to be a decorator like Lauren?"

"Who's Lauren?" I asked.

His mouth opened slightly and he shifted his eyes. "Oh . . . uh." His voice changed. "If you're looking for your dad, he's inside the house, in the kitchen area."

"Thanks."

Lauren? I'd never heard the name before.

Dad was standing at the roughed-out sink, poring over blueprints. He looked up. "Hey, sport. What brings you here?" He gave me a quick hug.

"Bored. What kind of countertop is this going to be?" It extended around two sides.

"Marble."

"Wow. Expensive."

"I know, but the buyers wanted the upgrade. So as long as they're willing to pay . . ."

"Who's Lauren?" I asked.

"Who?" Dad was clearly caught off-guard. "Oh, *Lauren*. She's the decorator for these houses. Furnishes a model to give prospective buyers a better idea of how great the house will look with carpets, furniture, and all that stuff."

"Dad, I understand that. What I want to know is, do you *know her?*"

"Well, sport, of course I know her."

"How well?"

Dad bent over the blueprints. "Pretty well. We've gone out a few times."

"You have?" I felt a strange little lurch.

My voice must have reflected my shock because Dad looked over and gave a little laugh. "It shouldn't come as much of a surprise that I'm seeing someone. Your mother, after all, has a boyfriend."

That seemed different somehow. Steve was a known factor, while this Lauren person had come out of nowhere. And just when I'd been about to ask Dad if I could come live with him!

I sensed that this wasn't the right time to bring up that subject. I'd wait until I found out more about what was going on between Dad and this woman. Maybe all they did was talk about the houses and the best way to show them off.

"Let's go outside," Dad said. "I need to talk to Sam."

We had no more than stepped over the still unfinished doorsill when Dad said, "What do you know? Here comes Lauren now."

I turned and squinted against the sun. What

I saw, blurred, was a tall, slim brunette in tapered slacks and a rib-hugging top making her way around piles of dirt as she walked toward us.

"Hey, there!" Dad said as the woman drew close. "I was just telling sport here about you."

"Sport, it's so nice to meet you."

"My name's Hannah," I said.

"Hannah. I love that name. It was my grandmother's." She smiled and extended her hand. "I'm Lauren."

Reluctantly, I shook hands. She was a looker, I'd give her that. She had straight, shiny dark hair caught by a barrette before it streamed halfway down her back. I couldn't see her eyes behind her huge dark glasses, but I found out later they were a rich chestnut color.

"So what's the story?" Dad asked her as we started walking again. "Did they ever deliver those chairs?"

"Tomorrow. Right now I've got two different window treatments. Would you have time to go over and give me your opinion?"

Oh, right, I thought. *My father's such a curtain expert.*

But to my surprise, he said, "Sure. I need a break anyway. Want to come along, sport?"

"How far is it?"

"Just down that way." He pointed to a finished house around the curve. "The model, you know. You've been in it."

"Yeah, well," I said. "I've got to get going. So I'll leave you two." Meaning *You two probably want to be alone.*

"No need to rush off," Dad said. "Surely you can give us a few more minutes?"

"No, really." We had reached my bike, and I got onto it. "See you later, Dad," I said. And then politeness forced me to mumble, "Nice to meet you, Lauren."

"It was really good to meet you, Hannah. Maybe one of these days we could all have lunch? Get acquainted?"

"Uh-huh."

"Maybe some day early next week?" She looked at Dad.

"Okay by me. How about you, sport? All booked up?"

Very funny. He knew very well I was at loose ends. "Yeah, okay," I said unenthusiastically.

Dad turned to Lauren. "How about bringing Jesse along? I'll bet he'd really hit it off with Hannah."

"Jesse's your dog?" I asked, hoping it was.

They both laughed. "Jesse's her kid," Dad said. "How old is he now, Lauren? Twelve?"

"Next month. But old for his age. Too old."

Too young to interest me, I thought. Why would a thirteen-year-old want to hang with a kid who hadn't even turned twelve?

"Bye," they called, walking off. I barely heard my dad say, "She's not usually like this."

I couldn't hear Lauren's reply, but I did notice she took hold of his hand.

Well, I thought, *it looks like I'll be putting a hold on asking Dad to let me come live with him.* I could tell by the way they'd looked at each other and by something in their voices that they were more than just business friends. It made me feel sick. It wasn't too surprising, but still, I never dreamed my dad would get a girlfriend.

As I pedaled away, I began to feel furious. What right did she have to call me Dad's special name, sport? How much did she know about me? What had Dad told her?

Well, I knew one thing: She'd learn nothing from me because I wasn't going to be around her. As for having lunch with her and her kid . . . forget it. It wasn't going to happen.

It did, though, on Wednesday of the very next week.

three

"Why are you wearing those grungy old jeans?" Melody asked that morning. "You look like last week's laundry."

"I'm just going over to the building site," I said, lying a little.

"So? Don't you have any pride? You're the boss's daughter, don't forget."

"Who cares?"

"I do," Melody said. "As much as I regret it, you're my sister, and how you look reflects on me."

"Don't claim me as your sister, then," I said. "I don't claim you."

"Why are you in such a rotten mood? I realize that the only two friends you have in the world are out of town, but even so." Melody finished drying herself from the shower, tossed the towel on the floor, and reached for her underwear.

I wasn't really looking, but still, the blue and red caught my eye. "What's that?" I gasped just as she pulled up her underpants.

"What?"

"On your rear."

"It's a parrot. Can't you tell?"

"I mean, is it a *tattoo*?"

"Baby, it's not a decal." She stepped into her jeans and lay on the floor so she could pull up the zipper.

"When did you get it?"

"A couple of weeks ago. Tiffany got one, too. A swan."

"Does Mom know?"

"Of course not, geeko. And you'd better not tell her."

"Are you kidding? I don't even want to be around when she finds out."

"I really don't know why she should care. It's my butt."

"Tell *her* that."

Melody stood, put on a silky shirt, and sucked in her stomach as she shoved the tails into her jeans. "Just shut up, Hannah. Okay?"

"Okay."

"What do you want, anyway?" she asked. "Why are you in my room?"

I'd almost forgotten. "Did you know Dad has a girlfriend?"

"It's about time he got a life." Melody leaned toward the mirror to examine a possible flaw on her chin.

"I'm meeting them for lunch."

Melody whirled around. "And wearing *that*?"

"Great," I said. "All you care about is looks. It doesn't bother you that our father is dating a bimbo?"

"Bimbo, huh? Like a stripper or a topless waitress?" She was probably teasing, but I couldn't be sure.

"Oh, come on, we both know Dad better than that. By bimbo all I meant is that this woman is . . . that she's . . . well, she's younger than Dad." I considered this. "Younger than Mom, too, I'd guess."

"Get real, Hannah. You want Dad to date someone from the senior center? What does this woman do for a living, if anything?"

"She's a decorator. She's doing Dad's model home at the moment."

"Hey, great! Maybe she could give me some cool tips on how to redecorate this room." Melody picked up her hairbrush. "I'm so sick of this cutesy floral decor I could vomit."

It was just like my sister to see how she could profit from any given situation. "There's something else," I said. "She has a kid. A boy."

Melody perked up. "How old?"

"Eleven. Almost twelve."

"Oh." Fast fade. She bent over and brushed her hair from the bottom to give it more body. "Anyway," she said, her voice coming from down under, "you should wear something that's clean, for starters. And something with a little pizzazz, if she's a decorator. What's her name?"

"Lauren."

Melody straightened up, her face a little pink, and brushed her hair into shape. "Is she good-looking?"

"I guess so." I left the room and changed my T-shirt for a yellow top with embroidery. I kept on the same old jeans instead of the new pair that I was saving for when school started. I wasn't out to rack up points with this woman.

I told Dad on the phone that he didn't have to pick me up, that I'd bike over to the restaurant.

"That's good," he said. "It'll give me time to finish up here. Lauren's picking up Jesse."

So the kid was going to be there! I hadn't

thought I'd meet him this soon, if ever. Well, I thought later, pedaling through town, he needn't think he's going to be my little buddy. I'd give him the chill treatment from the start to let him know he wasn't going to make it with our family.

I saw at once, though, that Jesse seemed no more charmed to meet me than I was to meet him. We scarcely glanced at each other when we were introduced. But quick as it was, I saw that I was taller by several inches and that the only unusual thing about him was his large black-lashed green eyes.

We didn't look at each other again, not even when we were seated at the square table. He was on my right, but we could have been on separate ice floes.

I'd somehow expected this boy to be in awe of me, older as I am, but this didn't seem to be the case. He was plainly just not interested. What gall!

It's hard to snub someone who seems to be unaware of you. I decided what I needed to do was make him admire me tremendously and then, when he was in my power, slap him down to size.

The waitress took our drink orders and then handed out menus. I stared at mine, although I already knew I'd order my favorite at this restaurant—thin-crust pizza with tandoori chicken.

When Jesse put down his menu, I decided to pretend interest in him just to get his hopes up. "I suppose you're a Bulls fan," I said.

"Why do you suppose that?"

I was a bit taken aback. "Well . . . most Chicago guys are."

"This is a suburb of."

What a jerk. Here I was, trying to be nice . . .

Dad looked up. "You guys ready to order? Jesse?"

The waitress had appeared, open pad in hand.

"I'll have the tandoori chicken pizza," Jesse said.

I couldn't believe this. Of all the things on the menu!

"And you, Hannah?"

Of course I had to switch. "Club sandwich," I said. Too late I remembered Melody's advice: "Never order spaghetti or a club sandwich or anything hard to eat like that on a first date." But this wasn't a first date or any date at all, for that matter.

Still, I'd wanted to impress this kid with my cool, and that would be very hard to do battling a three-decker with squishy tomatoes and mayonnaise squirting out the sides.

After Dad and Lauren ordered, Dad looked at me. "Hannah, Jesse is quite a sports fan, too."

And to him, "You've got tickets for the Bulls this year?"

"Yeah. My father gets them every year. We don't make it to every game, though."

I almost gasped. I'd never been able to go to a game, and here he was, being so nonchalant. *Yeah, we have tickets, but hey, sometimes we don't even go.* Plus, he'd just led me to believe he wasn't a Bulls fan. I loathed him. I loathed him a lot.

Lauren gave me what she probably considered a charming smile. "Your father tells me you're quite the soccer player."

And how much else has he told you? I wondered. "I do okay."

"Okay?" Dad all but barked. "You're the top player. Everyone knows that, so don't be modest."

Was he trying to score points with Lauren through my soccer game? If so, I wasn't going to cooperate. "I don't think I'll go out for it this year," I said.

"What?" Dad was startled. "Why not?"

"I'm tired of soccer. I'm going out for debate instead." Where *that* came from I don't know.

Lauren leaned forward. "I think that's wonderful, Hannah. Kids should try all kinds of things while they're young." She turned to Dad. "Isn't that right, Richard?"

Before he could pull together a reply, Jesse interrupted. "Could I get another Coke?"

His mother frowned slightly, but Dad signaled to the waitress. "How about you, Hannah?" he asked.

"I'm fine."

Dad pointed to Jesse's glass and the woman nodded and walked away. There was a bit of an awkward silence. Then Dad, acting as the go-between, turned toward Lauren's kid.

"Jesse," he said, "we haven't heard about your experiences at camp."

"Like what?"

Dad kept the smile. "Like, did you see any snakes?"

"A few. Five or six."

From the glance at his mother and the way he pulled his teeth over his lower lip, I sensed he was lying.

"What kind of snakes?" Dad asked.

"Lots of different kinds," Jesse said.

"Name them," I said, to call his bluff.

He looked directly at me. "Grace, Minnie, Candy, Gail, and George." His green eyes didn't blink.

"Really, Jesse," his mother said, smiling.

"Okay. The last one was really named Harry. But I called him George."

So he had a sense of humor. I might have warmed toward him if he'd been someone else.

Lauren then told about visitors' day at camp and how it was so much fun she wished she could sign up and stay.

Yeah, right, I thought. *If it had been Camp Elizabeth Arden.*

Turning to me, she asked, "Did you go to camp this summer, Hannah?"

"No." A wicked impulse made me add, "Mom couldn't afford it."

Dad flushed and Lauren looked embarrassed. "Maybe next year," she said.

I shrugged. There was a long silence, and then the adults started talking about the model home. Jesse gave me a sidelong look I couldn't read. Did he think I was a jerk or did he halfway admire my rudeness? I couldn't tell.

"What kind of computer do you have?" he suddenly asked.

"Me? I don't. But my mom has one."

"What kind?"

"Beats me."

Jesse simply stared, as though I were beyond ignorant.

"You going into sixth or what?" I asked.

"Seventh. At Jordan Junior."

"You are? But that's my school!"

I half expected him to say "You don't own it," but I guess he hadn't picked up on my tone. "I hear it's pretty good. For a public school. My dad would rather I go to boarding school."

"Why don't you?"

He gave a little twist to his lips. "Mom's against it."

I glanced at her and wondered if she got along with her ex-husband. She happened to glance at me at the same time and gave me her practiced smile. What was her agenda? Did she hope that Jesse and I would hit it off and help her weave a web around our family?

Dream on, I thought. *It isn't going to happen.* I didn't much like this kid, and I also had definite doubts about his mother. Although I knew my mom and dad would probably never get together again, I wasn't ready for either of them to make new attachments.

And it came to me once more: What about me and Dad, our closeness? And what about my idea of moving in with him? Was that now on hold or had it become out of the question? But surely this woman didn't have a strong grip on my dad. Not yet, at least, since he'd never even mentioned her before the other day.

I knew what I had to do: Save my father from making a huge mistake in relationships. And Lauren had to be a mistake, since she came complete with one very obnoxious son.

four

Cheyenne called from somewhere in Michigan Friday night to report that she was terminally bored, being stuck in the same car and then the same hotel room as her brothers.

"You know what they did last night, when we were supposed to be in our room?" she asked. "They sneaked out into the hall and took all the breakfast order cards people had put on their doorknobs and switched them around."

"Even your parents'?"

"Are you kidding? They don't order room service. Maybe they *want* to, but it costs too much. But they should, you know? Because it's so disgusting the way my dog brothers chow down. It's like a natural disaster the way they demolish the breakfast buffet."

"Get off my phone," Melody said, coming into the room from the bathroom, hair dripping.

I paid no attention. She always made a fuss, even though Mom had said from the beginning that I should use Melody's phone rather than tie up the family line. There was another line besides, for Mom's business, but that was definitely off-limits.

"What's that noise?" Cheyenne asked.

"Melody's hair dryer." I motioned for my sister to go back into the bathroom, but she ignored me.

We talked for quite a while, interrupted many times by Cheyenne's shouts to her brothers to stop doing whatever it was they were doing. "Got to go," she suddenly said. "They're writing obscenities on the mirrors with soap, and you know who'll get the blame."

"See you soon," I said, and we hung up.

To my surprise, Melody, hair mostly dry, was leaning against her pillow, picking at her nails in a halfhearted way.

"Aren't you going out?" I asked. "It's Friday night."

"No, I'm not, because Keith's mad at me."

"How come?" I settled back on the other twin bed.

She let out an exasperated breath. "Just because he saw Jeff hug me. Like, what's the big deal? We used to go steady, before I met Keith. You'd think Keith would feel good about another guy still wanting me, even though I blew him off after I met Keith."

"Uh-huh."

Melody changed the subject. "How come you squids aren't with Dad? As you so cheerfully pointed out, it *is* Friday."

"He had a meeting with the permit people."

Melody laughed. "You believe that?"

"Why wouldn't I?"

"Think hard. Since when do housing officials meet on weekend nights?" She lifted a foot and crossed it over her bent knee, the better to examine her toenail polish. Purple. "Dad may have a meeting, but I'll bet it's with you know who."

When I didn't reply, she continued, "What did you think of her, the decorative Lauren?"

"So-so. Do you think Mom knows about her?"

"Of course. She's not living in mystic space-land. Mom knows more than she lets on, at least to us."

As Melody shifted her legs, I saw a flash of underpants under her long T-shirt, which reminded me of the tattoo. "Melody, tell me the truth. Who did your parrot, a man or a woman?"

"Man."

"And you let him see your underpants?"

She laughed again. "I wore my swimsuit. The skimpy one."

"So he saw your butt."

"What do you think? That he did it with his eyes closed?" She picked at another toenail. "Anyone on the beach sees just as much if they care to look."

That was true. Her glo-orange suit has a thong back about as wide as dental floss. I don't think Mom knows she has it.

"If you don't have any more probing questions, why don't you go somewhere and stop cluttering up my room?"

I looked around at the real clutter—clothes, towels, magazines. I pointed toward an empty soda can. "You should recycle that."

"And you should recycle yourself out of here. Now."

The phone rang.

"I'll get that!" Melody lunged toward the table and picked up the receiver. "Who is this? . . . Oh, *Keith*," she said, as though she hardly remembered him from her mass of admirers. "I was about to leave, but I can spare a few minutes."

How did she learn to handle guys like that? I wondered as I left the room. Where did she get her training? Not from Mom, certainly. Mom would have told the guy to go take a hike. Maybe it was a genetic thing Melody had inherited from a femme fatale ancestor.

The next day, when Dad picked up Paige and me, I considered asking him how the meeting had gone last night. I couldn't do it, though. If he'd fibbed and really was out with Lauren, I didn't want to know about it.

"I take it Melody's busy, as always," he said. My sister considers herself too old to be picked up like a parcel, or so she says. As I mentioned, she almost never goes out with us anymore, but instead arranges impromptu meetings with Dad when she has nothing better to do, or when she wants to ask him for money.

Paige gave a huge sigh. "Sometimes I just don't know what to do with that girl. Her social life drives me over the edge." Paige often mimics adult talk—usually, as in this case, Mom's. It might sound cute coming from a four-year-old, but at eight, Paige is pushing it, in my opinion. No one says anything, though, so why should I?

"Daddy," Paige said, in her real voice, "I can't believe that I'm really going to see all those cats!"

Last year when she found out I'd gone to the

cat show with Cheyenne, she'd thrown such a fit that it brought on an asthma attack. This year, ever since she had seen the ad in the paper, she'd given Mom no rest. "So," Mom said to Dad on the phone, "since you'll have the girls on Saturday, you might as well take them to see those blasted cats. Even if Paige gets sick, at least we won't have to deal with her hysterics."

Now Dad was stuck with Paige and any problems that might develop.

"Just remember the rule," he said as we drove. "No touching, no petting."

"You're not supposed to anyway," I said. "The breeders don't like it. You could give their cats germs."

Once we got to the cat show, Dad paid for our admission and we went into a huge room, almost like an airplane hangar. It was filled with aisle after aisle of cages.

"Now, let's all stay together," Dad said. "I don't want to have to find you in this crush of people." He took hold of Paige's shoulder. "You hear?"

"They put lost kids into cages," I said.

"I wouldn't care if there were kitty cats with me," Paige replied.

The first aisle we wandered down featured longhairs. The cages looked like covers of romance novels, with tiny four-poster beds, lace curtains, and swags of roses. I wouldn't have been surprised to hear a feline version of Scarlett O'Hara meow, "Why, I declare. Such a fuss!"

Suddenly a voice blared from the loudspeaker: "Numbers sixteen and twenty-eight, come to show-area number four at once. This is your last call."

A young woman whipped past us with a cat so covered with black puffed-up fur you could hardly see its face.

We reached the end of the row and came to one of the judging areas, this particular one for Persians. The woman we'd seen with the black cat shoved it into cage number twenty-eight and then took a seat, the last one.

"Let's watch," I said to Dad. I liked to predict the winning cat. It was hard, though, because they all looked so perfect. Last year I'd found that each breed had qualifying points on features such as bone structure, shapes of eyes and ears, and so on.

The judge, a rather large woman wearing a top with sequined cats printed all over it, took a gray cat out of the cage and set it on the white enam-eled table in front of her.

"Good density," she said, lifting the cat up and down. "Solid, but not overweight." She pulled its ears back and stared into its face. "Eyes nicely rounded. Flat features."

After judging the creature's alertness by fanning a peacock feather in front of its face (this one couldn't care less), the woman put the cat back into its cage and went through the same procedure with the others.

When she'd picked the winners and the owners had come forward to retrieve their darlings, we moved on to the next area, where the judging had already begun.

These were Manx cats, I could tell, because they had no tails. There was one empty seat at the end of the row, which Paige took. Dad and I sat behind, with him on the aisle.

The judge was a man, who was remarking that the cat had good flared ears and fine markings.

I was distracted by Dad, who suddenly turned sideways in his seat. I looked and saw Lauren coming near. When she reached us, she leaned down to whisper something to Dad.

I could feel my face flaming with anger. Why was she here? Couldn't she stay away from my father for just one day, when he was supposed to be with us?

Paige turned around and stared at them, then looked at me. I folded my arms and kept my gaze fixed on the judging, though I didn't hear a word of what was being said.

Dad and Lauren moved away, and Paige popped back to sit next to me. "Who's that?" she whispered, confused. I shook my head as if I didn't know.

When the judging was over, Dad and Lauren joined us.

"Hannah, how nice to see you again," Lauren said to me. She looked a little flustered. Before I could reply, she went on, "And this must be Paige. How are you, sweetie?"

"Okay," my sister said in her pretend-shy voice.

"This is Lauren," Dad said. "A decorator and a friend of mine."

"Oh," Paige said, clueless.

"How come you're here?" I blurted.

Lauren seemed not to notice my abruptness. "Believe it or not, it's because of a client." She smiled. "He wants to surprise his wife with a cat on her birthday, and he wants a pedigreed one—nothing but the best. So I'm here checking out the breeds."

"You should get a white cat," Paige commented. "They're the best."

"Maybe you're right." She exchanged a brief

amused look with my dad. "But what kind of white cat? That's the problem."

"I could help," Paige said. She was really taking in the woman and liking what she saw. "I'll go around with you." She held out her hand, and Lauren, beaming, took it.

What a pushover, I thought, as Dad and I followed along behind them. Paige shines up to anyone who gives her the least bit of encouragement. I wondered if this was really a chance meeting or if Dad and his girlfriend had set the whole thing up.

We separated for a moment and then caught up with Lauren and Paige at a cage where they had stopped to admire kittens. A For Sale sign was attached to the cage. "You could take the gray and white one, and I could take the all-white one," my sister was saying.

"Paige, honey," Dad said, "no cats. You know the rule."

"But Daddy!" Paige had tears in her voice. She turned in appeal to Lauren.

"She's terribly allergic," Dad explained. "The only pet she can have is a goldfish."

"I did have one, but it was floating on top of the water in its bowl, dead. We had to flush it," Paige said, real tears now appearing.

Lauren turned to Dad. "Couldn't she have an outdoor cat?"

Great, very helpful.

"I'm afraid it wouldn't be outdoors for long," Dad said.

We moved on, with Paige dragging, giving mournful looks at the kittens.

"Have you been upstairs?" Lauren asked when we got to the end of the aisle. "They have great cat things up there. Sweatshirts, jewelry, toys—"

"Oh, I want to see them!" Paige said, hopping from one foot to the other.

Lauren glanced at her watch. "I really have to leave. But maybe just for a few minutes . . ."

The upstairs was like a fair, with booth after booth of cat stuff you wouldn't believe. Paige planted herself in front of the jewelry, all with cat motifs, and ended up getting a bracelet and ring. I couldn't tell if Dad was relieved about being able to make Paige happy at last or if he was just playing up to Lauren.

"How about you, sport?" he asked, turning to me. "What would you like?"

"Nothing," I said, to be aloof, although the watch with the cat hologram was really cool. Cheyenne would kill for it.

"Sure?" He paused. "Maybe we should pick up something for Melody."

"Dad, get real. She doesn't like tacky jewelry." I knew I wasn't being very nice, but this whole situation—sharing Dad with Lauren on our day—had put me in a bad mood.

Pretending not to notice, Dad said to Lauren, "My eldest daughter prefers Tiffany."

Lauren laughed. "Who wouldn't?" I noticed that her gold earrings gleamed like the real thing, and the chunky bracelet just above her watch must have cost a mint. "I really must leave," she said. "It was such a pleasure running into all of you like this."

Dad couldn't take his eyes from her as she walked away.

I turned to take a last look at the cat watch.

Dad noticed. "You're getting it," he said, pulling out his charge card once again. "I insist."

I caved. "Okay." I wondered if he'd ever bought his girlfriend jewelry. He had never given Mom anything after the time she'd taken back a pearl ring and bought a breadmaker and some crystal glassware with the money.

The next afternoon, after Dad dropped us off at home, Paige rushed to Mom, seated on the sofa with the Sunday papers. "Guess what? I saw a lot of cats and almost held one and didn't sneeze even once. So now I guess it's okay if I got an outdoor cat."

Mom glanced at me. "Where did that idea come from?"

I shrugged.

"It came from Lauren," Paige piped up. "I'll bet she'd let me get one." She flopped onto the sofa and folded her arms, face defiant.

"You don't know that she would," I said, aware of Mom's grim look. "You met her for what? Ten minutes?"

"Well, she's nice. Very nice!"

"Anyone," I said, "can be nice for a small stretch. Come on, let's go wash our hands. I guess dinner's almost ready?" I looked at Mom, who was not pleased by this conversation. She didn't reply, so I started off with Paige.

"Stay here," Mom said to me. "Paige is able to wash her hands without your help. Paige, go. Now!"

I stood, rooted, wishing I were somewhere else. When Paige had finally dragged herself off, Mom said, "How does it happen that you were with that woman?"

"We ran into her, accidentally, at the cat fair."

"Accidentally on purpose? Can't my daughters be with their father for one brief weekend without her—!"

"Mom, I really don't think they planned it." Why was I sticking up for them, when the two of them together might ruin my plan to live with Dad?

"All right." Mom snatched up the scattered papers. "Go set the table. For four."

"Melody's home?"

"Melody is not home. Steve's coming over."

I went to the kitchen to get the dishes and couldn't help thinking that to Mom it was okay for Steve to hang around. Big, gruff Steve who got along with everyone. He even stood up for Melody and treated Paige like a delicate little vase. As for me, Steve didn't have a lot to say. I guess I'd made it clear, without actually meaning to, that my own dad was my pal.

Now, though, was that about to change? Dad had treated me as always today, and yet I'd felt edged out when Lauren had appeared. Was she becoming more important to him than I was? Could that possibly happen? I'd do my best to see that it didn't.

five

Mom's business telephone began ringing. "Oh, wow," she said, getting up. "I hope they've located that trucker. I lost him somewhere in Idaho."

"They don't give you time off at all," I commented.

"How can they? The trucks have to go through regardless."

I followed and watched as she answered the phone and then began hitting keys on her computer. Images that meant nothing to me appeared on the screen.

"Got him!" Mom said into the phone. "Thanks, Roger. I can track him now." She hung up and kept working.

"Those guys are lucky," I said, "getting to drive all over the country."

"Not so. All they see are truck stops and factories. And the occasional bar, I suspect, although that's strictly against regulations." She moved the mouse around. "Go finish setting the table, please."

While I was putting the napkins out, Melody rushed into the kitchen from outside. "Oh, good," she said, noticing the set table, "you haven't eaten yet. Where's Mom?"

"In her office," Paige said, joining us. "Where have you been, young lady?"

"Out."

"Out where?"

"Stuff it, Paige."

Mom ambled into the kitchen. "Oh, Melody, you're here." She went to the window as we heard a car pull into the driveway. "And here's Steve."

I set another place as Mom went out to greet him.

Melody muttered, "If he calls me kiddo one more time . . . !"

They came into the house and Steve smiled his genial smile. "So how are the kiddos tonight?"

"Just peachy," Melody said under her breath.

"Okay," I said, managing a smile.

Paige ran to Steve for the traditional hug. "Guess what? I went to a cat show and almost held a kitten!"

"No way!" From Steve's expression you'd think she'd driven a team of huskies over the frozen North. "What kind of kitten?"

Paige looked to me for help.

"English eccentric," I improvised.

"I'm impressed," Steve said.

Paige always pushed to the limit. "And that's not all. I met Lauren!"

"The movie star?"

"No!" Paige giggled. "The lady Daddy knows. And I got this cat ring." She held out her finger for inspection.

In a bored tone Melody said, "Are we going to eat, or what?"

"It's all ready," Mom said. "Sit down, everyone, and I'll put it on the table."

To my relief, Steve took over the dinner conversation. He was going to Springfield to the state fair and asked Mom if she'd like to go along.

"Don't I wish," she said. "But the job . . ."

"Girls?" Steve beamed at the three of us. "Plenty of room. I'm taking the van."

"I'd rather be chopped off at the knees," Melody said.

Mom glared at her, then said, "The two little ones couldn't go, then, either."

Little one? Was I a *little one?* I didn't think so!
"Anyway," I said, "I promised Grandma Orrington
I'd spend some time with her before school starts.
We've made plans." Actually, I wanted to wrap
that up before Kelsey and Cheyenne got back.

"But thanks for asking," Mom said, and nailed
us with a look.

"Yeah, thanks," we all said.

I really do love Grandma Orrington, Mom's
mother, and felt a little guilty that my drop-in
visits this summer had been so brief. But she's
busy, too, working part-time at a crafts shop, so
it wasn't as if she'd been hanging out the window watching for me. She had Monday off this
week.

She picked me up at about ten. Paige whined
a little because she wanted to go along, but
Grandma said, "Now, honey, you've been at my
house several times, and I need to spend some
quality time with Hannah."

Paige's lip trembled. "What am I supposed to
do here all alone?"

"I suggest you weed the garden. Or help your
mother with the laundry," Grandma said firmly.
She loves Paige, of course, but never gives in to

the near-tear routine. Grandma called out good-bye to Mom, and we went out to the car.

"She acts like such a baby," I said, as we pulled out of the driveway.

"Because she gets away with it," Grandma said. "Now, Hannah, what are your plans for the coming school year?"

"I may go out for debate." I stole a glance at Grandma to see how that played.

"Debate? What a good idea. Develops your reasoning skills."

That sounded like a downer to me. Like algebra.

"It makes you look at both sides of a question. Depending on the draw, you can argue for the affirmative or the negative."

"I know." I did?

"It's like the law," Grandma went on. "If the attorney is hired by the defense, that's the route he goes. If he's a prosecutor, he finds reasons to prove the person guilty."

"Well, who decides whether the guy is or not?"

"The judge, or the jury—after all the arguments, pro and con, are in."

Fortunately we had come to road construction, so my grandmother had to concentrate on getting past all the big machinery. Grandma is very nice, but I have to say she sometimes tells you more than you really want to know about a subject.

"What have you been doing lately?" I asked after we'd passed the roadwork.

"The usual things. Growing my flowers and vegetables. Remind me to give you a bag of zucchini when you leave. They're taking over the back yard."

"I thought you just gave us some."

"I did. And to all my neighbors. Still they keep coming."

"How's everything at the crafts shop?"

"Fine. We're getting in some new fun things. Oh, and you may be interested . . . I have a quilt in a frame at home."

I couldn't visualize a whole quilt framed, but when we got to the house it was something entirely different from what I expected. The quilt was rolled partway, held by clamps in a big contraption sitting on sawhorses like the ones Dad uses sometimes in building.

"You roll up a section at a time," Grandma explained, "and then quilt that section."

I looked and saw tiny stitches going around the colorful pieces. "You do those?" I asked.

"My friends come over and help sometimes," she said.

"But it must take so long!"

"Yes, but what's the hurry?" Grandma sat on a straight chair in front of the quilt and examined some of the stitching. "You've heard of quilting bees?"

"I guess. But I never exactly knew what they were."

"It's an old-fashioned term. In the old days there weren't that many things for women to do, outside of work around the house. So they'd get together and quilt and talk and gossip."

"Could I try?"

"Of course." Grandma brought over another chair and I sat beside her. "Here's the needle . . . notice how small it is . . . that's so you can make small stitches. You put one hand under the quilt so you know you're stitching all the way through the quilt."

I tried. "Ouch! I stuck myself!"

"You learn to feel the needle without actually drawing blood after a while." She laughed as I looked at my finger and saw a tiny drop forming. "It's an art, like everything else. Now, what do you say we have lunch?"

She had made a fruit salad. With it, she served cottage cheese and toasted raisin bread, my favorite.

"Paige wants to get an outdoor cat," I said, as we started eating. "You know, one that stays outside."

"And where did she get that idea?"

"From Lauren." I was testing now. "Dad's friend?" Did grandma know about her? I wondered.

She didn't react, which made me think she'd heard about the woman. "Why does Paige think a cat would hang around?"

"It probably would, if she fed it."

"Where would it go in the winter?"

"Maybe into the playhouse. What do you think?"

"It's not up to me, it's up to your mother. Are you ready for dessert?"

"Sure."

While we were eating the brownies and ice cream, Grandma said, "Melody stopped by the other day. She's growing so tall."

"What did she want?"

"To see me, I assume. I'm glad she wants to touch base now and then. We had a nice talk."

I was a little surprised that Melody actually took time out of her demanding social life to pay Grandma a visit. I wondered if she confided things the way I did. Last spring I'd told my grandmother about Ray Janson kissing me under the bleachers after a soccer match. Grandma said, "Well, you have to start somewhere."

No way would I have told Mom. She'd have sewn a scarlet letter on all my clothes.

Grandma had continued, "So, do you like this boy?"

"Not really. He's kind of a jerk. But I liked the kiss."

She smiled. "Well, why not?"

Now I casually asked, "What did you and Melody talk about?"

"The usual. What's going on in her life. And she showed me her new ink."

"Her what?"

"Tattoo. I gather that's what the in-crowd calls them. At least she didn't get a pierce. Those disgusting things they clamp onto their navels, eyebrows, nose, and so on."

"She'd better not. You don't know my mother." And then we both laughed. Of course Grandma did. Since she was a baby.

Picking up the dishes, Grandma said, almost to herself, "She has no reason to talk anyway."

"Mom, you mean?"

Grandma only gave a small grunt. I was dying to know what scenes my mom had played out when she was a teenager, but I knew Grandma would never tell. Well, maybe she would when I was grown.

That night I called home to see if Cheyenne or Kelsey had tried to reach me. Melody answered the phone. "No one called for you," she said. "Mom's gone out with Steve, and I'm stuck baby-sitting." She yelled to Paige, who was protesting in the background. "Oh, stop whining. You *act* like a baby."

"Tell her I want to talk to her about getting an outdoor cat when I come home tomorrow," I said, feeling a bit sorry for my little sister.

"Tell her yourself," Melody said. "As for you, we're through talking." She hung up.

It seemed to me that Mom and Steve were seeing more of each other than ever. Did this mean that Steve was getting closer to becoming my stepfather? Or was it only Mom's way of showing Dad that he wasn't the only one with a love life?

Whatever it was, I didn't like it. Steve was easy enough to take, provided he didn't become a per-manent fixture around the house. I didn't need another dad.

But what about my actual father? Where was

he headed with this girlfriend of his? How far had they actually gone?

The thing that distressed me, that made me nervous, was the way my dad and Lauren acted. I could see no signs of just-getting-acquainted awkwardness. They seemed very comfortable with each other.

It bothered me more than I wanted to admit. The closer they grew, the more squeezed out I'd be.

I wished they'd break up. Maybe they would. Adults, I'd noticed, were very unpredictable. If they did split, Lauren would probably feel bad for a while. But she had that kid.

As for Dad, he'd always have me. We could go back to being pals, the way we'd always been.

six

"Were your trips wild and crazy?" I asked Cheyenne and Kelsey when we got together on Wednesday.

"No, I'd have to say for the most part mine was boring," Kelsey said. "The baby got a rash and then a fever, and we spent too much time at a pediatrician's."

"But other than that," I urged.

"Other than that, we drove forever and stopped now and then at scenic places that I've already forgotten."

"How about you, Cheyenne? Did you have any fun at all?"

"Not possible. Being trapped with my brothers was like being in solitary confinement."

Kelsey cleared her throat. "Cheyenne, solitary confinement means being *alone*. You know?"

"Of course, and I was. Alone with my brothers. Most of the time."

"Did you take any pictures?" I asked this partly out of politeness. Other people's photos taken at who knows where are usually huge yawns.

"Yes, but we don't have them back yet," Cheyenne said.

With Kelsey it was the same. "My folks won't pay extra for the one-hour option."

Their downbeat attitude got to me. At least they'd been away somewhere, while I'd been stuck at home the whole summer.

"But still, you were together as a family," I said. "Even if my mom and dad had been able to take time off from their jobs, we'd have gone somewhere split up."

I guess I sounded more mournful than I'd intended. Both nodded and then Cheyenne said, "It must be tough, with both of your parents divorced."

We stared at her.

"What?" She blinked. "Oh, okay, I get it. They'd both have to be, wouldn't they?"

"Duh," Kelsey and I said in unison.

They'd brought over their school schedules, which had arrived while they were gone. We compared. Kelsey and I had a different homeroom from Cheyenne, but we all had the same lunch hour and, of course, rode the same bus.

"Guess what," I said. "I may sign up for debate."

"Eeeee!" They both looked at me as if I'd said I was going to shave my head.

"*Why?*" Kelsey asked.

I tried to reconstruct the situation with Lauren and Jesse, but it sounded feeble even to me.

"You could always say it was a brain lapse and you've thought better of it. Or maybe they've even forgotten," Kelsey said.

"I told me grandmother, too. She thinks it's a giant step in my development."

"Oh, yickkk," Cheyenne said with sympathy. "What's this Jesse like? Tall, dark, and the usual?"

"Shorter than I am, dark, and a seventh grader."

"Yickkk!"

"I know. And a smart-ass besides."

"Make him disappear," Kelsey suggested.

"Don't I wish."

The night before school was to begin, Paige walked into my room even though I'd put up a sign that read CURSED BE ALL WHO ENTER HERE!

"Get out," I greeted her. "Didn't you see the sign?"

"I don't understand it." When I explained, she replied, "It's a sin to curse." Then with a sigh she said, "I'm just so scared, I don't know what to do."

"Scared about what?"

"New grade. That means I'll have a new teacher."

"It's that way every year unless you flunk."

"But Ms. Attison was so nice."

"The new one will be nice, too," I said, looking through my closet, trying to decide what to wear for the first day. I settled for something old rather than any of the new stuff I'd got, so I wouldn't look too eager to impress.

"And my friend Nicole said today that Mom will probably marry Steve and then I'd have a new father. I don't want a new father. I like my old one."

I sat on the edge of my bed and pulled Paige down beside me.

"Mom and Steve probably won't get married. They just like to hang out together." I said this to calm Paige down, not because I really believed it. "Come on, let's go to your room and decide what you'll wear tomorrow."

It made Paige, with her attention span of minus zero, forget everything else. But as I looked through her outfits, the thought of Mom and

Steve kept surfacing. And when they'd paired off, what about the other couple?

"This one, definitely," I said holding out a floral top with matching pants.

Paige eyed it critically. "No, I like the blue," she said.

So much for my sisterly input.

I was already on the bus when it picked up Cheyenne the next morning. She was wearing a hot-pink top with rhinestones spelling out the word "girl." Since Cheyenne has no sense of boundaries when it comes to clothes (her mother is just as bad), she took the boys' remarks and the girls' hard stares as total admiration.

Even when Dede Klein, across the aisle, murmured, "Tacky," Cheyenne just smiled before scooting next to me.

"Oh, look, Rick is getting on," Cheyenne said. "He's the one with the T-shirt."

"They're all wearing T-shirts," I pointed out, but still there was no mistaking the hunk.

"Yo, Chey," he said as he walked past us down the aisle.

"Yo, yourself," she replied.

"How do you know him?" I asked, impressed.

"He was buying a six-pack of Pepsi at the convenience store when I walked in, and so I bought Pepsi, too, although I'd really gone in to buy a pound of unsalted butter. I mentioned to Rick that it was quite a coincidence, both of us buying Pepsi. 'Like kismet, that's fate,' I told him."

"It would have been a real coincidence if he'd also gone in to buy unsalted butter. There's Kelsey!" I waved.

She came to our row and told Lisa, who was across the aisle, to scoot over. Most kids would have let Lisa keep the aisle seat, but Kelsey took no prisoners. "Move," she insisted. The girl did, glaring.

Kelsey swung her legs to the aisle and leaned over to talk. Every time new kids got on the bus she had to move. Eventually, the driver yelled, "Keep that aisle clear back there." But that was okay. We were almost at the school, Jordan Junior High (named for an architect, not the basketball player).

Inside, Cheyenne split for her homeroom and Kelsey and I headed down the hall. I was in the middle of saying, "What are you doing after . . ." when I suddenly stopped. There was that kid, Jesse, just closing his locker! He didn't see me.

"After?" Kelsey prompted. "After school, you mean?"

"Uhhhh . . ."

"What's the matter with you?"

"Nothing. I was just . . . distracted . . . for a minute." I didn't want to acknowledge Jesse. I wouldn't even speak his name. I hated to think about running into him every day.

That night Dad called to see how we'd coped with our first day. Melody, of course, wasn't home. I kept my conversation on the "okay" level. Paige, totally forgetting her idolized teacher of last year, now raved about her new one. "And she likes me, too," Paige went on. *How did she know this? How was this message transmitted?*

Later, glancing at Mom, I asked Paige how she knew this teacher liked her.

"Because when Miss Thornhill said she knew this was going to be a wonderful year, she was looking smack at me."

"So be wonderful," I said.

"She always is," Mom remarked, with a fond look at her darling. "And you're going to get me that bumper sticker again this year, aren't you, Pixums?" Pixums nodded. The bumper sticker proclaimed: I'M THE PROUD PARENT OF AN HONOR STUDENT AT ADAMS ELEMENTARY SCHOOL.

I had always tossed away the sticker each year because my thinking was, Why should Mom brag about my grades to the universe when she didn't make a fuss at home?

The one time Melody hit the honor roll (the planets must have been in alignment), Mom all but lit incense and beat a gong. Melody had remarked, "Mom, get a grip. You never carry on about Hannah."

Mom had looked startled. "Because she's always on it."

"But you never say anything."

"Hannah knows she's a good student."

"Oh," Melody said, "and I'm not?"

"Sure you are," Mom countered. "If you'd just try." Melody never tried again. She even crossed out the word "Honor" and wrote "Rotten" on the sticker. When Mom finally noticed what it said, she scraped it off.

That night when I went to bed, I remembered the announcement that had come over the loudspeaker at school. *All students who wish to sign up for extracurricular activities must do so this week. If you fail to do this, you must then get approval from your counselor.*

Maybe I could conveniently forget. And not have time to meet my counselor. But wouldn't it make me lose face with Lauren if I didn't sign up?

Not that I really cared about Lauren. It wasn't that. But still, I did want her respect, for what it was worth. And besides, knowing my grandmother, I wouldn't get away with the lame excuse "I forgot." She expected me to live up to whatever it was that I was supposed to live up to.

Okay, I thought, turning off my lamp. *I'll sign up for debate, but then I'll find a reason to drop out.* I had no ideas at the moment, but surely something would come to mind.

Then I remembered what Grandma had said about debate developing reasoning skills. Now, that was something worthwhile. If I could just learn how to promote arguments for the side I was on, it could prove valuable in my proposition to Dad about my going to live with him.

I hoped I'd pick up some pointers . . . fast. The way things looked, I wouldn't have a lot of time before that romance of his closed the door and shut me out.

seven

The announcement was repeated at school the next day, as though no one had listened the first time. Actually, most kids do ignore the loudspeaker unless their names are mentioned.

At lunch I groused about signing up to Kelsey and Cheyenne. "I guess it comes down to a choice," I told them. "Either pretend I was just blowing air or register for the stupid thing and suffer in silence."

"Silence?" Cheyenne inquired. "But isn't debate, like, a talking thing?"

Kelsey, who has learned to glide over most of Cheyenne's off-the-wall remarks, said, "You'll have to do it or lose face. It couldn't be that bad, anyway. It might actually be fun."

"Then why don't you guys sign up for it?"

"Okay," Cheyenne said.

"Don't I wish." Kelsey reached to the floor for her backpack. "As I mentioned, I've been nailed to pick up the baby from daycare every afternoon and take over until Mom gets home from work."

"That's so not fair," Cheyenne said.

"I know, but what can I do? As the folks pointed out, it'll save a few bucks, cutting down baby-care hours. Bucks translates to a bigger allowance."

"In that case," Cheyenne said, "you should do your share." She thought. "Maybe I should offer . . . my brothers . . . ? But no, definitely not. There's not that much money in the world."

When Cheyenne and I strolled into Room 201 for debate team, we were the first ones there. Mrs. Waltermire, who also taught math, greeted us with, "Ah, new recruits. Hannah . . . good! You have a logical mind. And Cheyenne . . ."

"I know, words fail," she said with a laugh. I'll say this for Cheyenne, she more or less takes herself as she is.

As others wandered into the room, we rearranged the chairs into a circle. I happened to glance up and then sharply sucked in my breath.

"What?" Cheyenne looked from me to the boy I was staring at. "Who's he?"

For a moment I was struck dumb. Then I managed to mutter, "That's the kid!"

"Of what?"

"Of Lauren."

"Who's—? Oh, I remember. Your dad's new squeeze."

"I'm leaving."

"No, you can't," Cheyenne said, taking hold of my arm. "Besides, he's already seen you."

In fact, he was walking toward us.

"So you really did sign up," he said in his superior way. "I thought you were just blowing air. To impress my mother."

How did he know? "I never try to impress," I managed to say with dignity. "I don't feel the need." *Lie!* Then, "This is Cheyenne."

"As in Wyoming," she said. "And you're . . . ?"

"Jesse, of course." He said it as if he assumed I'd discussed him with my friends.

"Oh, and here comes Space Ship," he remarked, as a totally weird number appeared. "You see before you the prime example of a bad case of moonburn."

The girl, spying Jesse, walked toward us. Her hair, copper-colored as a plumbing part, was highlighted with dripping green strands around her face. "These are?" she inquired, giving us the eye.

"Cheyenne and Hannah."

She shrugged and walked off.

"What did you call her?" Cheyenne asked. "Space Ship?"

"Yeah, because she's circling out there somewhere."

"Will you all take seats?" Mrs. Waltermire called out above the buzz. "What a wonderful turnout. I can see that we're going to have a lively debate season! To get started, please go around the circle and say your name. You start," she said to the girl seated next to her.

They got past Cheyenne and finally reached Jesse and his very strange friend.

"Jesse Marshall," he said.

"Space Ship," the girl muttered, while everyone stared.

"No nicknames, please, no matter how picturesque."

"Wanda Wurlitzer," the girl said through gritted teeth. "But I'm called Space Ship by those who don't want to experience pain."

Our leader's eyelids fluttered. "Next," she said.

When we'd gone around the circle, Mrs. Waltermire said, "Today I'm going to explain how a debate team works. I see a few members who were here last year. Would you raise your hands?"

There were only three.

"Where are the other bodies buried?" someone said, just loud enough for Mrs. Waltermire to hear. She pretended not to.

"I'm going to divide you into two teams," she said. "Then I'll assign a topic. One team will be pro, or for the topic, and the other con, or against. Then each group will huddle and come up with arguments. Count off now, saying pro or con."

It came as a shock to many of us, as we counted off, that we'd be opposed to our friends sitting beside us. Cheyenne and Wanda were united on the con side, and I was a pro with Jesse!

"Can't we stick with our friends?" one girl objected.

The teacher eyed her. "There are no friends in debate. Just team members and opponents. Our first topic is this: Should students be required to wear uniforms to school?"

It was clear from the looks of distaste, backed by groans, that no one wanted to argue in favor of uniforms. We separated and went to different parts of the room.

Wanda Space Ship stayed with Jesse.

"Hey, wait a minute," a kid named Trent said as he eyed her. "Aren't you supposed to be on the other team?"

"I'm supposed to be where I choose to be. You have a problem with that?" she said, practically in his face.

Trent backed away. "Way cool."

"So!" Jesse said. "Shall we proceed?" To our collective amazement he produced a leather case and unzipped it to reveal a laptop. "We'll toss around ideas, list the valid ones, and then prioritize."

I was thunderstruck. Who did he think he was, taking over this way? But when I looked at the others, they all seemed to take it for granted that he was in charge. I wasn't going to cave, however. "Just a minute," I said. "Who made you the leader?"

Jesse eyed me for a few moments and then said, "We'll take a vote. All in favor of my heading the group say aye."

All of them except me were on his side.

"Any further comments before we begin?" Jesse asked.

"Yeah," Space Ship said. "I'm not going this route. Uniforms suck."

"So go over to the other group where you belong anyway," Jennifer Alvarez said. She flinched at Space Ship's glare. "Or stay."

In an effort to assert myself, I said, "Uniforms could be positive because they free up time you'd waste by wondering what to wear."

"Good point," Jesse said, as if I were looking for his approval. He entered it into the laptop.

"Yeah, you could spend the time blading," a skinny kid—Roy—said.

"Only geeks do inline," Wanda Space Ship said.

"And also," Trent added, "it's an outdoor thing and mostly for summer."

"We're straying from the point," Jesse said. "Any other reason why wearing uniforms would be a good move?"

"You don't have to compete with other kids for drop-dead looks," Amy said. "Not that I do."

"That's obvious," Shelley said, eyeing Amy's lame outfit.

"Cuts down on clothes competition," Jesse mumbled as he recorded. "What else?"

Really resenting his takeover attitude, I stayed silent while the others piped up with arguments.

Finally Mrs. Waltermire clapped her hands the way they used to do in kindergarten to get kids' attention. "That's all we have time for today. We'll continue this next time. I can hardly wait to hear what you've come up with."

"My lunch," Wanda Space Ship muttered.

Jesse hit a few keys and snapped shut the case. "I'll print this out and copy you guys when I see you in the halls."

"How do you know you'll see us?" Shelley said. "I've never laid eyes on you before today."

"Then give me your fax number."

As we stood, mouths agape, he continued, "No fax for any of you? Not to worry. We'll work something out." And he and his spacey friend strolled off.

"Get him!" Jennifer said. "Who is this guy, anyway?"

"Who cares?" Roy said. "Let him do the work."

To my chagrin, Jesse was waiting for his bus when Cheyenne and I arrived on the scene.

"Has Space Ship taken off, then?" Cheyenne stared at the sky. "Oh, I think I see her, trailing fumes."

Unperturbed, Jesse remarked, "I hope your team has a grip. We've lined up some winning arguments. Haven't we, Hannah?"

I shrugged and looked away.

"We don't have to try very hard," Cheyenne said, "because no one is in favor of uniforms anyway."

Jesse smiled. "That's not how it works. Here comes your carrier. *Arrivederci.*"

"What an obnoxious know-it-all!" Cheyenne said as we took our seats. "I'm glad *I'm* not related to him."

I gave her a sharp look. "Are you saying I am?"

"Well, you could be, you know, if your dad—"

"My dad wouldn't do a stupid thing like marrying Jesse's mother."

"And you base that on what?"

"I don't know," I mumbled. "I just don't think he would."

"Oh, okay. Maybe you're right. Look, here comes Rick. I wonder why he's taking the late bus."

Rick sat across the aisle from us, and Cheyenne babbled away at him until she got off. I didn't mind that her attention had refocused. I didn't want to talk. What could I say anyway?

I was so sorry I'd talked Cheyenne into joining debate. It would make it that much harder for me to drop out.

I'd have to do it, though. Being on the same team—in the same room, for that matter—with Jesse was more than I could take. Anyone could see that.

eight

Melody and I were watching TV Friday night when Mom drifted into the room wearing a full-skirted dress I'd never seen before. But Melody focused on her feet. "Are those *cowboy boots?*" She asked in her most put-down manner.

"A version of," Mom said. "Like them?"

Melody just continued to stare, so I said, "Red. Hot color, Mom."

"Steve's taking me to a country-western bar. I may even learn the two-step."

"Oh, please." Melody turned back to the TV.

"Mom, you look great," I said. "And nice earrings." They were turquoise, to match her belt.

She looked pleased. Mom had had a tough time after the divorce. I think she didn't really want it, but never came right out and said so, at least in front of us. I don't know what the problem was. Anyway, it was nice that now she was enjoying herself.

Paige came downstairs just as Steve arrived and he and Mom were getting ready to leave. "Where are you guys going?" she asked.

"Out," Mom said.

Paige folded her arms. "Young lady, I want you home by midnight. I don't care if it *is* Friday night."

"Funny," Mom commented.

Steve played along. "Yes, ma'am, I'll get her home in good time." He smiled. "But you don't have to wait up for us."

After they went out the door and Paige was in the kitchen, Melody murmured to me, "If it were Saturday night and you two were with Dad, hard telling what time she'd roll in, if at all."

I stared at her. "What do you mean?"

"Oh, grow up. What do you think I mean? They think I don't know."

In a little while the doorbell rang and Paige ran to see who it was. "It's the Chinese take-out," she called.

"Money's on the table," Melody said.

In the kitchen we pulled the warm cartons out of the bag. "Black bean shrimp," Paige recited, opening them. "Moo shu pork, lemon chicken. Rice. But there's no beef."

"Live with it," Melody said.

We all filled our plates. "Don't you want lemon sauce on your chicken?" I asked Paige. "I thought you liked it."

"Not now."

When we'd finished, most of the chicken was still on Paige's plate.

"You shouldn't have taken so much," I said, "if you didn't want it."

"I'm just saving it. For later." She scraped it onto a paper plate.

After putting the leftovers in the fridge, I went upstairs to use Mom's phone; I wanted to call Kelsey in private and get her up to speed on the debate thing.

"Now, remember, Kelsey, anything I tell you is private," I reminded her. "Don't blurt out our strategy in front of Cheyenne."

"Like it would register anyway," she said. "Heard any more from that smart-ass Jesse?"

"Not since he 'copied,' as he calls it, all of us."

We were interrupted by the sound of her mother shouting.

"Gotta go," Kelsey said.

Melody came to the door just as I hung up.

"Keep an eye on Paige. I'm going out." I wondered if Mom knew about it, but there was no way I was going to ask and get Melody in my face.

The house was quiet, really quiet. I checked Paige's room, but she wasn't there, nor could I locate her downstairs. Even the TV was off. Had she sneaked off to her friend Nicole's house? It wasn't like her to do that. I went to the patio and called her name.

I saw a faint glow, as from a flashlight, in the playhouse. Why would she be there now? I crossed the yard and just as I reached it, a yellow cat streaked out, leaped to the fence, and was gone.

"You scared him!" Paige wailed as I stooped to look inside. There were paper plates strewn around and what looked like the breaded parts of the lemon chicken.

"How long have you been feeding that cat?"

She shrugged. "I don't know. But it keeps coming back. It likes me. At first it ran away as soon as I came inside, but now it knows I'm its friend."

"Paige, why would you do this? You know you're allergic."

"I don't think I'm allergic to this particular cat," Paige said. "But sometimes I wear this." She held out a peach-colored disposable mask she must have pilfered from the doctor's office. "For times when I'm feeling wheezy but need to be with the cat."

I sighed. "You don't *need* to be with it."

"Yes, I do. I need it for my happiness." She clicked off the flashlight. "Don't tell Mom about the cat."

"You can tell her yourself when she drives you to the emergency room with an attack."

This Paige shrugged off. "Know what I call my cat?" Suddenly it was *her* cat. "I call her Butterfly."

"Butterfly? *Butterfly?*"

"Because she just flies over the fence!"

"I see. Let's go inside. But pick up those paper plates and put them in the trash or you'll have ants all over the place."

As we returned to the house, I said, "You know, Paige, that cat is probably someone's pet."

"I know, but he likes me best." *It,* then *she,* now *he.* Paige covered all possibilities.

I made her wash her hands and face, even though she protested that she couldn't see any fur clinging to her.

"How was your western night?" I asked Mom at breakfast the next morning.

"Super. I didn't realize how much fun country-western music could be or that Steve was so into it. He tried to teach me all the steps . . . even got me into line dancing . . . but I was pretty much of a klutz."

"Next thing you know," Melody said, slathering butter on her pancakes, "he'll come rattling around here in a pickup truck with a gun rack."

"Oh, Melody," Mom said. But she was smiling.

A little while later Dad stopped by for Paige and me. Before we left, Mom made Paige go upstairs and change her top because there were syrup stains on it.

"How's your project coming along?" Mom asked Dad. "Want some coffee?"

"No, thanks. We're winding up work on most of the houses. The developer's getting ready to stage an open house." Dad didn't sit down, but kept jiggling the coins in his pocket and looking up the stairs. "Where's Melody?"

"Off somewhere. You just missed her."

"She's always off somewhere. Would you please tell her I want to spend some time with her?"

"Tell her yourself," Mom said, heading for her office.

As we were driving away, I asked if the model

house was finished, too. I guess I was hoping that Dad would lose interest in Lauren if they didn't see each other every day.

"It's almost ready for prospective buyers to come see," he said. "Lauren's over there today, wrapping everything up."

"Can we stop by?" Paige squeaked. "I'd just love to see Lauren again! And besides, I have a secret surprise to tell her."

Dad smiled, obviously pleased. "All right, honey, but just for a few minutes. Then we're going to the nature center. You like that place, don't you, girls?"

"It's okay," I said. I'd rather have gone into the city. One of these days I was going to arrange to be alone with Dad. If Melody could do it, so could I. I certainly couldn't hint around about living with him if Paige was there, taking it all in.

When we reached the model home, I saw they'd put in landscaping and finished the driveway. It almost had a lived-in look. All it needed to be a true example of suburbia was a tangled hose, a Big Wheel in the driveway, and a basketball hoop above the garage door. We pulled up behind what must have been Lauren's car.

The door was halfway open. Dad called, "Hello!" and Lauren came into the hallway, smiling in surprise. "I didn't expect you—uh—any of you," she amended as Paige and I appeared. "How nice. You can give your opinion of my latest." She led us into the kitchen and pointed to a series of framed pictures of fruit she'd just hung. "Too artsy?"

"Looks good," Dad said, as if he knew.

"You going to put those up, too? As a balance?" I asked, pointing to others still lying on the counter.

"I don't know. What do you think?" She held up two on the other side of the window.

"I guess I would." I really guessed I didn't care one way or the other.

"Okay. Will you help me?" She swept back her long hair, which hung loose today, with a yellow headband to match her summer-weight sweater. I honestly didn't think she'd expected to see us, or anybody, but her makeup was perfect. She was even wearing high heels instead of the sneakers most women put on when they're doing stuff around the house. But, of course, this wasn't her house and she was far from being your ordinary housewife.

I strolled away, thinking she didn't need my

help or anyone else's, but Dad and Paige got into it.

After a while they all came into the front hall, where I was standing. "Want to see the children's rooms upstairs?" Lauren asked me.

I shrugged, not only because I wanted to leave but also because I felt lukewarm about seeing still another Star Wars–inspired room. Decorators all seemed to take it for granted that that's what kids wanted.

I started up the stairs, with Paige following. She suddenly pulled at me, and when I turned she put her hand over her mouth, giggled, and whispered. "Look. Dad and Lauren are kissing!" I glanced down into the hall below and my heart gave a lurch. They were, like, glued together.

"Who cares?" I said, rushing upward. I wished I didn't.

We went past the master bedroom, then walked farther down the hall to a child's room with—ugh—clown decor. Paige entered, but I spied another room jumping with rock star posters, a flame-colored comforter, and, against a wall, a stereo system. As I walked in, a slight noise made me turn toward an alcove, and I gasped. Jesse was seated at a computer!

He turned. "Hey, what are you doing here?"

"I . . . uh . . . we . . . just stopped by."

"You look in shock."

What could I say? I thought of something. "I'm really surprised . . . you know . . . to see a computer."

He stared. "It's only my laptop. You've seen it."

"Oh, right." *Jesse must think I'm dense.* But better that, I thought, than to admit his presence shook me up.

He turned back to the computer and hit a few keys. "I'm trying to log into yesterday's congressional debate . . . Oh, here it is."

If he expected me to fall apart in admiration, too bad. "So long," I said.

He swirled around. "Hey, what's your hurry? We ought to talk."

I didn't think so. "What about?"

"The debate gig. I think we have a pretty good team."

I shrugged.

He went on, "Not like some of those twits who're on the other side. Like that Cheyenne-as-in-Wyoming, for starters. She's a genuine ABCOM."

"What? What does that mean?"

"A Bad Case of Moonburn. You know."

"No, I don't."

Jesse sighed. "It's like she's been out under a full moon too much of her life. Moonstruck. Loony."

"Listen, Cheyenne's one of my very best friends!"

Jesse shrugged. "Fine."

"And speaking of loonies," I went on, "What about *your* friend, Space Ship? She's in full orbit. You even said so yourself. As for being moon-burned, she's baked."

"Yes, but only temporarily. Some day soon Space Ship will go back to being just plain Wanda. But your friend will always be the way she is."

I was so angry, I wanted to shove him right off his swivel chair. Instead, glaring, I said, "I have two questions for you."

"Shoot."

"Why does she let you call her Space Ship? Isn't that a bit degrading?"

Jesse smiled. "Not in her mind. She thinks it means she's way above ordinary people, high-tech."

"Second question. Why do you hang with such a loser?" *Being so above it yourself?*

"To annoy my father."

"What?"

Jesse leaned back and rested his hands behind his head, like some kind of executive. "You see, Hannah, my father, being an attorney, is into negotiation. He does it at work, he does it with me."

"I don't get it."

"When we disagree, he gives a little, I give a little. We come to terms. Example: He wants me to study a foreign language in the summer. I don't. So I take the course, and he buys me an upgrade on something electronic."

"That's just plain bribery."

"Call it what you will, it works for us."

I turned to leave, but stopped. "How does Wanda fit into your negotiations with your father?"

Jesse stretched. "He disapproves of her, of course. So one of these days he'll make me an offer."

I stared at him. "Are you saying you're just using Wanda to get something out of your dad?"

"Bingo. You grasp the concept."

"You . . . you're despicable!"

He shrugged. "You asked, I told you."

Through my disgust I managed to ask, "Why

did you choose Wanda as your target person?"

Jesse smiled. "While she's not the prime kook of her coven, she looks as though she is, and that's what my dad would react to. Looks. He's very keen on making the right impression." He elaborated. "His clothes are always very expensive, very smooth, but they don't attract attention. You just know he's someone who looks very capable of handling things."

Except for his son, I thought. Jesse really had his father snowed. I'll bet his dad thought he could solve any problem by throwing money at it.

I left without another word.

When I got to the stairs, I saw that the others were already in the hall.

Smiling, Lauren asked, "Is Jesse still at that computer?" And then my angry look registered. "What's the matter?"

"Nothing. Can we go, Dad?" I walked past all of them and went outside to the car.

When he got in the car, Dad asked, "What's the matter, Hannah? Did Jesse say something to upset you?"

"He said a lot, but I don't want to talk about it."

"Well, I think we should. It's best to air disagreements, settle them."

"There's nothing to settle," I said. "Jesse is a spoiled, egotistical . . . jerk! And I hope I never have to be around him again!"

"Well," Dad said. "Well."

Paige sighed, and in Mom's voice said, "Honey, I know just how you feel."

"No, you don't," I said. "So please shut up."

nine

I usually don't see Kelsey or Cheyenne over the weekend because of being with Dad. This Sunday night he brought us back a little earlier, though, because I really needed to finish up some homework. First, I told myself, nail the math assignment, and then as a reward make a call.

I was only about halfway through when Kelsey gave me a buzz. Did I tell her to call back later? Of course not. She was fired up with great news.

"You'll never believe this!" She seldom sounded so breathless. "I was blading past the park, where the guys shoot baskets, you know?"

"Yeah."

"And I stopped and watched. Then they were leaving, and something dropped to the ground. I picked it up and it was a foreign coin, a big one. So I bladed up and asked whose it was, and Aaron turned and said, 'Oh, that's mine.' Then he gave me the cutest smile and said, 'Keep it. It's yours.'"

"How much is it worth, do you know?"

"That's not the point! Aaron gave it to me. *Aaron.* i'll keep it forever! In fact, you remember that What If game we played? Well, if the question came now, about the most precious possession I'd save, it would be the foreign coin Aaron gave me."

"You're demented." Aaron, from the little I'd seen of him, was one of those guys who combs his hair a lot but makes sure there's one little lock brushing his forehead. He must think it makes him look like one of those teen TV actors.

Finally Kelsey asked, "Anything new with you?"

"No. What did Cheyenne have to say about debate? I don't mean strategy," I hastily added. "Just in general."

"All she mentioned was the strange girl called Space Ship. Hard to believe she's a friend of your friend."

"Jesse's not a friend. He's disgusting. Stuck-up, no morals. Materialistic."

"But other than that?"

Without thinking, I blurted out, "He's an ABCOM."

"Which is?"

"A Bad Case of Moonburn."

"Oh, an acronym of. That's cool. How did you come up with it?"

What could I say? That I'd appropriated it from Jesse, who'd labeled Cheyenne an ABCOM? "Don't repeat it to anyone, okay?"

"I don't even know the kid." In the background I could hear the baby crying and Kelsey's mother yelling, "Get off the phone and pick her up!"

"See you tomorrow," I said hastily, and hung up.

ABCOM, moonburned. I had to agree, much as I hated to, that Cheyenne was a genuine ABCOM. Loony for sure, but still lovable. And Kelsey? Borderline moonburned, I'd have to say, in her own peculiar way. Had I selected Cheyenne and Kelsey as best friends to provide some color in my life because I was so colorless myself? I could even go on and label Melanie and Paige as borderline cases, too, but at least I'd had no choice in the sister selection department.

With my math concentration now shot, I strolled downstairs to see if something new had suddenly materialized in the refrigerator.

Stooping, I checked out the shelves. Same old stuff. I took an apple and got some chips and headed back upstairs. Something else Kelsey had said lurked in my mind. And then I remembered. The What If game. *If your mom could save just one person . . .* Things had changed since we'd played that game.

It wasn't a question of saving people anymore. It was a question of who matters most these days. It looked like Mom was setting herself up with Steve. And if that was so, she probably wouldn't mind all that much if I split. She'd miss me some, of course, especially my help around the house. But Steve could easily take my place. He was doing chores for Mom already.

The more serious roadblock in my path to Dad was Lauren. If Dad kissed her even when there was a good chance of our seeing him, he was pretty far gone. And that was extremely bad news. Then add Jesse to the mix and it was a disaster. Big-time disaster. Something had to be done.

I was tempted, as I had in the past, to get Grandma's input on my home situation. But why, and how, could she give me an accurate reading? Besides, at her age, she didn't need to have this laid on her. I could even see her giving us all up and moving to Phoenix to be near her other daughter. My aunt Helen leads an orderly life out there. She thinks her big sister, my mom, is a bit on the wacko side. But maybe all sisters feel that way. I know I do.

I sighed and reached for my homework, which I always finish, no matter what. *Hannah, the steady one. Hannah, the good student.* Sometimes I wished I could be more like Melody, coasting along, not a care in the world. But I couldn't.

Don't ask me how, but Jesse managed to get copies of the ideas to our entire debate team. Handing me mine at my locker, he didn't even mention our meeting at the model house. And of course, I was ready to block it from my mind. He'd even assigned an argument to each member of the team, a really take-charge move. But I had to admit it made things easier.

We huddled before the debate to make sure each of us knew where to go with the contest.

Still, although our team delivered some solid arguments, we lost, according to Mrs. Waltermire. "Your arguments were strong, but lacking in conviction," she said. "I felt that some of you didn't really believe in a uniform dress code."

We were disappointed. I thought Jesse would be crushed that we'd been defeated after all his work. Instead he said, "Okay, first battle lost, but now we know the enemy."

Personally, there was one enemy I decided I'd like to know a whole lot better. Brandon Schmitt. I'd noticed him from the first, of course, since he was so cute, but I'd thought he was just what people call a pretty face and not much more. To my surprise, he turned out to be a very strong debater.

Jesse was still yackety-yakking. "The word is *focus*," he said.

To me, when it came to Jesse, the word was *bossy*, but I let it go.

Later Cheyenne shared with me her own unique view. "We won because our team struck the right blow for liberty. That's what Gettysburg was all about."

"*What?* What does Gettysburg have to do with it?"

"You know, like people should be free. And not have to wear uniforms, like the blue and the gray."

"Cheyenne, this may come as a shock, but the Civil War was not about having to wear uniforms."

"But after it was over, they didn't have to, did they? So then everything was okay."

I'd noticed that her team had all but fast-forwarded past Cheyenne, which had helped play a part in their victory.

"You should talk longer next time," I told her, putting team spirit before friendship. "You're very strong in your beliefs."

"Okay. How about the new topic, Should drugs be legalized? I really feel strongly about that."

We all did. Everyone wanted to be on the pro side, but Mrs. Waltermire said we had to switch, and my group had to be against the topic this time.

"She's nothing but a dictator," Space Ship complained. "Always barking out orders."

"It's debate rules," Jesse said.

"Which suck," Roy said. "I'm thinking, like, if they legalized drugs, they wouldn't have all these dudes getting rich by smuggling the stuff."

"Then tell *her* that," Shelley said as Mrs. Waltermire approached us.

"Problem?" she asked.

"Yeah," Roy said. "Some of us here think drugs should be legalized."

"That's good," Mrs. Waltermire said. "Secretly, you may hold an opinion, but in debate you're often called upon to argue against it anyway." She smiled. "Lawyers do it all the time. They might believe their client is guilty, but they fight to prove his innocence. Work on it." She smiled again and drifted way.

"I couldn't defend someone I thought was guilty," I said.

Jesse shrugged. "Then don't go into law."

"Would your father?" I fixed him with a look.

"If he had to. But as it happens, he's a corporate lawyer, which is an entirely different field." He turned to Roy. "Maybe it would help if you thought of debate as a practice field for winning arguments with your parents."

"Hey! There you go!"

It was time to leave. "Get your ideas down, and we'll discuss them next time," Mr. Takeover said. "We can get all bruised and bloody with this topic."

"Sounds good to me," Space Ship said.

I had to go back to my locker and was digging around for a book when a voice said, "Hello again."

I gave a sharp turn. It was Brandon Schmitt, the kid with killer looks. Why did he have to be on the opposite team?

"Sorry you guys lost today," he said. "Personally, you were outstanding."

"You think so?" I could feel myself blushing. To think Brandon Schmitt was complimenting me!

He fell into step as I walked down the hall. "You should switch to our side," he said. "And then we could send over that airhead Cheyenne to Jesse's team. She and Space Ship would make a great pair of bookends."

I should have defended Cheyenne, but like a wimp all I said was, "I don't think Mrs. Waltermire would let us switch."

"You could give it a shot," Brandon said. He lifted an eyebrow, shattered me with his smile, and walked away.

It would be so great to huddle with Brandon and beyond great to be opposite Jesse. Oh, man— if I were able to hack into his computer, I could do real damage to him and his team! Of course, I'd never sink that low. But why even think about changing sides? Mrs. Waltermire was such a stickler for rules, she'd never let us switch at this point.

I couldn't keep the Brandon encounter to myself, however, so I called Kelsey, home now on baby patrol.

"You talked to Brandon Schmitt!" she squealed. "Actually? He's so animal!"

I recalled the image of his perfect smile and the way he flicked back the dark hair that kept spilling down. "He's kind of cute," I said, trying to hold myself in check.

"Kind of! What did he say?"

"Just . . . oh, something about debate. He's on the other side. Cheyenne's team."

"Maybe you could get her to switch with you."

"I don't think so. Jesse—"

"Oh, that ABCOM!"

I wished she'd forget that. If it ever got back to Jesse that I'd turned his phrase against him, I'd feel like a sneak. "Jesse wouldn't trade me for Cheyenne. He was the one who called her an . . ." I couldn't say ABCOM. "An unfocused individual."

"Oh. And as team captain, Jesse makes these decisions?"

"Some. But that's okay. Let him do the work." To change the subject I asked Kelsey if she'd made any moves on Aaron.

"Only in my dreams." The baby began crying. "Oh, rats. She always cries when I'm in charge. Some day when we're grown up, I'm going to tell her how she ruined my social life—and in my crucial teen years, at that."

"She'll love you for it. Bye."

I heard voices downstairs and realized Steve was there. Again. I'd never kept count, but it seemed he was around more and more as time went by.

In my mind I could still hear Kelsey's baby sister crying. *What if Mom and Steve got married and had a baby?* No. Not possible. Possible, yes—Mom wasn't too old. But she wouldn't, I thought, unless it was for sure a boy. And you couldn't be sure.

I went down to help with dinner. Mom always wants me to, so she can have a relaxing glass of wine (beer for Steve) before the meal.

She wasn't relaxed now, though. I heard her say, "And you know what she yelled? *'Why not just put an electronic bracelet on my ankle and be done with it?'*"

"Who?" I asked.

"Melody. Who else?"

Of course. "Hi, Steve."

"Hi, kiddo." I wished Mom would suggest he cut the kiddo and call us by our real names, but she'd never do that. Her view would be that we should just get used to it. "How's everything?" he asked, as always.

"Okay. Is something burning out there?" I went to the kitchen and Mom leaped up to follow. She grabbed a skillet in which butter had melted and was now burning at the edges. "See what your sister did? Made me forget all about this." She tossed the skillet into the sink.

"Melody's not home, is she?"

"Of course she's not! When is she ever?"

Mom checked the oven. "I'll give it another fifteen minutes."

The table was already set. Mom had put out a small bouquet of purple asters from the garden.

I followed her back to the living room, where Steve was sitting, and flopped onto a chair. "I'm taking debate at school this year," I said to kill time until Mom cooled down. "There's a girl named Space Ship on our side."

Steve laughed. "That's her actual name?"

"No, it's really Wanda. I think it's another way to get attention. She dyes some of her hair green."

"What do you debate about?" he asked.

"Next week it's should drugs be legalized."

"Drop out," Mom said. "You don't need to get into a drug debate."

"Oh, honey, she didn't say she believed in it," Steve said.

How long had he been calling her honey?

"Right," I agreed. "No one has to believe in it. It's just for the sake of argument."

Mom, clearly still steamed, said, "I didn't finish telling you about Melody, what she did." She paused, looking at Steve. "She got a tattoo. Without asking me!"

"Would you have let her?" he asked.

"Absolutely not!" Mom lunged forward to

straighten magazines on the coffee table. "But get this. She told her grandmother."

"Before or after?"

"After. But did she tell me? No!"

Usually I wouldn't say anything, but Steve's presence gave me courage. "As Steve just said, Mom, she knew you'd throw a fit."

Mom narrowed her eyes. "Did *you* know?"

"I happened to see it. Otherwise I wouldn't have known."

Mildly, Steve said to me, "You ought to confide in your mother, Hannah."

Noting my angry glance, he cleared his throat and then said, "I've been meaning to ask you, what kind of saw should I get to cut out some little wooden animals for my nephew?"

Clearly he was trying to get back into my good graces, but I was having none of it. "I wouldn't know," I said. "I'm not a carpenter. Just ask someone at the hardware store."

"Hannah," Mom said, "there's no need to take that tone."

"But she's right," Steve said. "I'll just drop in and see what they have."

I wanted out of there. "I'll go check the oven," I said.

"No, I will." Mom went to the kitchen and a

moment or two later called out, "Everything's ready. Hannah, get Paige, will you?"

At least I'd gotten her off Melody's case. I ran upstairs, but Paige wasn't in her room. I wondered if she could be out there with the cat again. I went downstairs, slipped out of the house, and hurried to the playhouse. As I suspected, Paige was inside, petting the cat. This time it didn't take off.

"You're not wearing the mask," I said.

"I think it scares her."

"It scares me to think of what'll happen if you get an asthma attack and Mom finds out why."

"But Hannah, I have to be very careful not to upset Butterfly. It looks to me like she's going to have kittens."

It looked a little like that to me, too. Why was it that every time you hear about stray cats they're about to have kittens? "Maybe you've just been feeding her too much," I said, hoping this was so. I didn't really want to think of where the kitten scenario might lead.

I told Paige it was in her best interests for the time being to keep mum about the cat. "Go change your top," I said. "And then hike downstairs. Dinner's ready."

I wished I knew a way to settle all this without

upsetting Paige and, more to the point, Mom. She'd probably blame me for not telling her about this either.

Mom didn't like things to go on behind her back. But was she being up-front with us about Steve? I didn't think so.

ten

"We've got to join forces," the voice said to me on the phone that night.

"Who is this?"

"Jesse." He said it as though I should instantly recognize his voice.

"Why do we need to join forces? And for what?" I asked.

"For debate. You and I are the only ones who have a clue. The rest of our teammates are foot soldiers, good only for following orders."

"So what are you suggesting?" I was interested to hear what he had to say, even though I didn't like the way he operated.

"Try to come up with some solid suggestions next week, and then we'll combine our ideas and assign arguments to the other team members. The opposition has some strong speakers. Brandon, for example, is a major player."

This was interesting. To me, the guy was strong but not that great. Or had I been focusing too much on his looks alone?

"Of course, on the debit side," Jesse continued, "they have that loose cannon, Cheyenne."

"Hey!"

"I know, I know. She's your bud. But admit it, her line of reasoning cannot be followed."

He was right about that.

"Someone on their team asked me to transfer to their side," I threw out, just to test Jesse's response.

"Who?" His tone was full of indignation. And then, when I didn't answer, he said, "Oh, I know. Your dim little friend Cheyenne."

"No. It wasn't Cheyenne."

"Who, then?"

"Forget it. It's not going to happen anyway." I wondered why winning on the debate team was so important to Jesse. Did it mean his dad would pony up another present? I also had to wonder if Lauren knew that her kid was a scheming machine.

Jesse got back to business. "We have a whole week to work up our arguments, because there's no school this Thursday, so no debate," he said. "How about coming over on the off day and we can do some strategic planning?"

"Why don't you come over here?"

"I don't think that's such a good idea. Better for you to come here."

To stall, I said, "I don't know where you live."

"I can give you directions. Or better yet, Lauren can pick you up."

Confused for a moment by the "Lauren," I said, "I'll see. Let you know later."

At school on Wednesday I ran into Jesse in the hall. "It's all set with Lauren to pick you up tomorrow at ten," he said.

"Ten?" I was searching my mind for an excuse to get out of it.

"Yeah, she has stuff to do later, and I have to meet my dad at around eleven. But don't worry, she'll drive you home."

Before I could pull my thoughts together, Jesse had walked off. At this point I didn't know how to get out of the meeting without a good excuse. Besides, I reasoned, Jesse and I had to get together eventually.

Had to? Why? Just because he said so? Still, I did want to win the debate, as a point of pride, I guess.

The only thing that bothered me was Mom's knowing that I was going to Jesse's. Every time Lauren's name was mentioned (and Paige went

into a rave routine about her once in a while),
Mom got that grim look on her face. I don't know
if it was the fact that Lauren is younger and . . .
yes, prettier . . . than she is, or if Mom just didn't
want any other woman in Dad's life. It didn't make
sense—but sometimes things don't.

So when Lauren called that night to confirm, I
told her I'd meet her on the corner.

In the morning Mom, hard at work at her
computer, only nodded when I said I'd be back in
about an hour.

Lauren was there, waiting in her Jeep
Cherokee. She'd mentioned she needed a car with
space to haul around design samples.

"Hannah," she said when I got in, "is it okay
that I'm picking you up?"

"Oh, sure," I said. I could feel her flicking a
look at me from behind her dark glasses, but I let
it go.

We drove into an exclusive part of town
called Tall Trees and down a curving street to a
two-story house, white, with pillars, that looked
really expensive.

"Here we are," she said. She got out of the
car, and I followed. The floor of the foyer was
white marble, and there were mirrors and
paintings along the wall. I glimpsed an elabo-

rate living room that looked like something out of a magazine.

"Excuse me a minute," Lauren said, and she clicked on an answering machine right there in the hall.

A business message came on first and then a voice that I recognized as Space Ship's.

"Jesse, you slimebag," she said, "I know what you're up to, but don't think you're just going to blow me off. I'll get back at you." That was all.

I hadn't noticed that Jesse had joined us. His mother turned to him. "What was that all about?"

He shrugged. "How should I know?"

"Who left that message?"

"A weird number called Space Ship."

"Space Ship? What kind of name is that?"

"I told you, she's weird. What more can I say?"

Jesse's mother looked baffled, but just then the phone rang again. It was someone calling about a decorating job. Lauren kept glancing at her watch and finally said into the phone, "Look, I'm running late. I'll get back to you."

To Jesse's obvious relief, she'd forgotten about Space Ship's message. "Jesse, be sure you're ready at eleven. You know how your father hates to be kept waiting."

"Time is money," Jesse said, in imitation of

what must have been his father's voice. "So see you later. Don't forget to come back and pick up Hannah."

Again, with just the tiniest of sighs, his mother looked at her watch and dashed to the door with a "See you later, Hannah."

Once her car had pulled out, I said, "Jesse, what did Space Ship mean by saying she knows what you're up to?"

"You tell me."

"What?"

"Well, someone must have tipped her off that I was just using her as a bribe factor with my father. You're the only one who knew that."

"Hey, listen," I said, outraged. "I'm not a sneak!"

"Okay, okay. Not important. Now, let's get to work. Come along." Over his shoulder he added, "It was probably that flake Cheyenne."

He could be right, I thought, following him. Maybe I'd said something to Cheyenne and Kelsey, and Cheyenne had passed it along. I honestly couldn't remember. We entered a room with two complete computer setups. One had fabric samples tacked onto a corkboard above it. Jesse pulled over a chair for me by the other computer.

"Here's how far I've progressed," he said, picking up pages he'd printed out.

Under the heading DRUGS SHOULD NOT BE LEGALIZED he'd entered the ideas we'd already come up with. "What else do you have?" he asked.

"Nothing." I sat there sullenly, arms folded. I might be stuck here with him, but I didn't have to cooperate.

"Nothing?" He turned to give me a look. "Then why are you here?"

I was asking myself the same thing. The truth was I loathed and despised this kid. I didn't want to be in this room with him, I didn't want to be on his team, I didn't want him anywhere near my life. But that was the problem. How could I get rid of him . . . and also his mother, if it came to that . . . without ruining my relationship with Dad?

Seeing that I wasn't going to answer, Jesse filled up the void. "The opposition will probably point out that liquor was forbidden in the 1920s during Prohibition, but that just made drinking go underground. So in answer to that, we say?"

I didn't reply.

Jesse went on. "We say that just because people flouted the law is no reason to give in."

Still fuming over the things he'd said, I just stared at him without expression.

It went on that way, with Jesse making suggestions and my not responding. After a while he just typed on the keyboard, pretending I wasn't there.

I was really relieved at the sound of the doorbell. "It's him," Jesse said. "Right on the dot of eleven."

I followed Jesse from the room. His father was waiting outside, and we joined him.

"Sir, I'd like you to meet a friend of mine," Jesse said.

His father raised an eyebrow. He seemed rather scary-looking, with his pointy beard and glinty eyes behind the glasses.

"This is Hannah."

"Hannah?"

"Hannah Pryor," I said. I didn't offer to shake hands and he didn't either.

"Ah." Now both eyebrows shot up. "The carpenter's daughter."

"Her dad's a builder, sir," Jesse said.

"And a carpenter," I added. "A great one."

"No doubt." The man's smile made me think of a lizard. "Jesse, we do need to leave. I have reservations at the club." I could tell he wasn't impressed by me or my dad, but that was all right.

We didn't need his approval. "Son, do you want to rethink what you're wearing?" He eyed the Smashing Pumpkins T-shirt Jesse had on.

"Actually, no. It's a gift from a friend."

Somehow I knew that this was part of Jesse's strategy with his father. He had probably bought the shirt himself to pretend he was still close to Space Ship. Maybe his dad would make the deal today. What a slick pair they were, Jesse and his father!

Jesse turned to me. "I'll be right back with a printout for you."

He went inside and his father went back to his Cadillac. I just stood at the front steps feeling awkward, wondering if the father was checking me out behind the tinted windows.

Just as Jesse returned, Lauren drove up. "Here it is," Jesse said, handing me a few pages. He hurried to his father's car, and they peeled out of the driveway. Neither of his parents gave any sign of the other's presence.

"Sorry if I'm late," Lauren said as I slid onto the front seat. "I guess you met the ogre."

I didn't know what to say so I kept quiet. "He never paid all that much attention to Jesse before the divorce," she said, backing out of the driveway. "Now he's very buddy-buddy."

"I guess he gives Jesse lots of things," I said without thinking.

"He does, and I don't approve of those tactics, but what can I say?"

I didn't think we should be having this conversation. Why should I get involved with their problems?

Lauren went on, "At least I'm happy to see you and Jesse getting along so well. He needs to be around someone with her feet on the ground."

I wanted to say that I had no need to be around Jesse. But Lauren began talking about her work then, just to make conversation, I guess.

Again, I asked to be let off at the corner. I'm sure Lauren realized why. "I shouldn't have made that remark about my ex-husband," she murmured apologetically. "I suppose I should be glad that he's finally spending time with Jesse."

I thought, *Spending time and money*, but all I said was, "That's okay. Thanks for the ride."

When I walked in, Mom said, "Oh, I'm glad you're back. I have to run over to the office for a consultation. Hang around, will you? The telephone company's coming to check out a faulty line. You can let them in."

"Okay." Paige's school wasn't off for the day, so I made a sandwich just for myself, then dialed Kelsey as I ate.

"Come on over," she said.

"I can't." I explained why. "You come over here."

"Huh! I'm stuck with the baby. Again."

"Why isn't she at daycare?"

"Because . . ." Kelsey's voice rose to imitate her mother's. "Why should I pay for the day when you're around, doing nothing?"

"Hmm. Hey, I know! Bring her over here!"

"There? Well, why not? Sure, I guess I could."

"I'll call Cheyenne to come over, too."

Cheyenne arrived first, all excited about being with the baby. Then Kelsey showed up, wearing her backpack and pushing the baby in its stroller.

"Well," Cheyenne exclaimed. "Here's the little mother!"

Kelsey glared. "Knock it off."

"Oooh, I want to hold her." Cheyenne reached for the baby, but couldn't get it out of the straps.

Kelsey reached down and pinched open the plastic locks that were something like airline seat belts. "Don't hold her that way," she said to Cheyenne, who had grasped the baby under the arms and was holding her aloft. "Sit down and hold her on your lap."

"Can I feed her?" Cheyenne asked, now seated.

"When she gets hungry. And then you can change her." Kelsey felt under the baby's diaper. "In fact, you can change her now."

She pulled a Pampers from her backpack and handed it over. Then she had to show Cheyenne how to put the baby down, undo the old diaper, and fit on the fresh, using the little plastic tabs. The diaper had pictures of ducks on the band.

"This is so great!" Cheyenne said, holding the baby once again as Kelsey took the wet diaper to the kitchen garbage can. I had a fleeting thought of Mom's total surprise if she happened to walk in and see a baby. "What's her name again?"

Kelsey made a face. "Babette. Can you see why we just call her Baby? If you give her the bottle now, she might sleep."

"Oh, great!" Cheyenne took the bottle and held it while the baby eagerly clamped her mouth on it.

"Tilt the bottle more or she'll inhale air and get gas," Kelsey said.

When half the formula was gone, the big sister said, "It's time to burp her. Hold her against your shoulder and pat her on the back."

When Cheyenne did as told, Babette gave a huge burp and dribbled formula on her shirt. Cheyenne didn't care. She gave the baby the rest of the bottle, burped her again, and then put her down on a blanket on the sofa. "Ooooh, baby, you're so sweet," she cooed, leaning over her.

"If you leave her alone, she may fall asleep," Kelsey said, to whom all this was old news.

The telephone rang, and I rushed to answer.

"Hello, Hannah? It's me, Brandon," the voice said.

"Oh . . . hi." I felt a little stunned, but thrilled.

"Have you thought any more about switching sides? In debate?"

"No. Besides, I can't."

"That's what I thought you'd say. I'm just calling to tell you it won't be necessary anyway."

Why did I feel let down? Had Brandon decided he didn't want me on his team after all? That I was weak or something?

"We're going to win. Without your help."

"Don't be so sure," I told him. Who did he think he was? I didn't care if he was a girl's dream of perfection. I didn't need his approval. "We've got some great arguments."

"Good. Go with them." He hung up.

Seething, I went back to my friends. "That was

big-shot Brandon," I said. "Bragging that his side is going to win the debate."

"Who cares about that?" Kelsey remarked. "Did he ask you to go out with him or anything?"

"No. And I wouldn't anyway."

"He hates Jesse, you know," Cheyenne said, adjusting the baby's blanket. "Just because he's a seventh grader, I guess."

"That doesn't make Jesse bad," I said. "We were seventh graders ourselves last year."

"I thought you didn't like him," Kelsey said. "And now you're defending him."

"I'm not defending him. All I'm saying is there are better reasons to hate Jesse."

"Oh? Tell," Kelsey said.

I didn't want to go into my reasons—I'd probably said too much already—but then Cheyenne piped up. "He's turned against his friend Space Ship," she said. "Jesse said he couldn't have her hanging around him anymore. Her image ruined his image." Cheyenne looked dreamy. "So now I've been giving Space Ship fashion tips. Or I should say *Wanda.* She's through with the Space Ship name."

"You're a great one to be giving fashion tips," Kelsey remarked.

"Oh, I know!" Cheyenne said, the sarcasm

blowing right over her. "But first I told her she had to lose the green hair. Nothing goes with that color."

I said, "Did Jesse give a specific reason for dumping her?"

"Not really. I think he just got tired of her."

"What a creep," Kelsey observed.

"That and more," I said, thinking that Brandon wasn't much better. I was beginning to think that all males were deceptive, but then I thought of my father. My father was one man I could always count on.

But could I?

eleven

At Dad's house on Saturday night, I decided to call home and try to catch Melody before she left, to see if there were any messages for me.

To my surprise, Mom answered.

"Hi!" I said. "How come you're home?"

"Because I am."

"Oh, Steve's there."

"Did I say he was?"

I was confused. Mom and Steve always got together on Saturday night.

"Why are you calling?" Mom asked. "Is Paige sick?"

"No, she's fine. I just wondered if anyone had called for me."

"Why? Who would be calling? Didn't you tell your friends you'd be at your father's?" Mom sounded annoyed. "Or maybe you were expecting a call from a boy? Don't tell me you're following in Melody's footsteps. I couldn't take any more of that."

She was in such a bad mood I wanted to ask if she'd had a fight with Steve, but I didn't dare.

My guess was right, as I found out from Melody after school on Monday.

"I don't know what it was all about," she said, "but as I came home on Saturday, Steve was pulling out of the driveway. Alone. He looked really upset. I would've asked Mom for the scoop, but she was in her room with the door closed. I felt really bad for her, but what could I do?"

"Knock, to see if she was okay?"

"No way. After about an hour she came to the door of my room and asked if I wanted to go to a movie. And that was weird, because as you know, we've hardly spoken to each other lately."

"So did the two of you make up and go?"

"I would've, but I had a date with Keith."

"Couldn't you have broken the date?"

Melody gave me an astonished look.

"It's possible, you know, to break a date," I said.

"It's possible. But I didn't want to."

That was so like my sister, always doing what pleased her, not caring about a little thing like consoling Mom.

At the next debate session, which began late, I had a good excuse to stare at Brandon because, as team captain, he made the opening remarks. He started out strong, saying that drugs should be made legal so there'd be no more point in smuggling the stuff across borders.

"We could get rid of the expense of border control agents because we wouldn't need them anymore," he said. "No laws would be broken. I know what you're going to say: 'Keep the drug laws and just beef up the patrols.' Forget it. It would take thousands of agents to cover the whole region."

Jesse and I exchanged glances. Beefing up the patrols had been one of our arguments.

Brandon rambled on and on, and then to everyone's relief, he finally concluded with a weak "It's the best thing, to make drugs legal. That's what I think. What my team thinks."

Jesse whispered, "Like we care what they think." But I could see he was a little unnerved.

He presented a pretty good argument,

though, for putting on more border patrols. "It'd be cheaper in the long run to hire guards than to track down drug dealers once they got into the country," he said.

That was a little off, because if drugs were legal, there'd be no need to chase down drug dealers. Jesse seemed to realize this, and he faltered a little. "I further say . . ." he stalled, trying to get his thoughts together. "I further say that it would be much better to keep our laws against drugs than to deal with the . . . with the . . . the terrible effects of having these substances readily available. To kids . . . to people . . . not that kids aren't people . . ."

The opposite team snickered.

"What I mean to say is . . ." Again he faltered.

Say it, say it, I thought.

"We could win the war against drugs by keeping them out of the country in the first place. And in conclusion—"

Our opponents suddenly broke out in applause.

"None of that!" Mrs. Waltermire said, and she snapped her fingers. "I'm afraid your time's up, Jesse."

"Thank you," he said, and sat down.

"What happened?" I murmured, trying not to move my lips.

"When Brandon said 'Beef up the patrols,' it threw me. That was going to be my opening argument."

It surprised me that a few little words could throw Jesse. To me he'd always seemed totally, obnoxiously, in control.

Friday night while I was watching TV, Mom came out wearing a killer dress, with the usual loose matching jacket to hide her no-longer-trim waist-line. "Like it?"

"You look great. Where are you going?"

"To a dinner theater."

"I didn't know Steve liked plays," I said.

"Steve? Who said anything about Steve? Believe it or not, I do have women friends." She sat down beside me. "What time is your father picking you up?

"In about half an hour."

"See that Paige is ready, will you?"

"Sure, Mom."

Unexpectedly, Mom put her hand over mine. "Hannah, I wonder if you know what a help you are to me, how I depend on you?"

"Ummm," I responded, eyes on the TV.

"You're always here when I need you."

"Uh-huh." I didn't know what to say. The TV image wasn't registering, but I kept my eyes on it anyway.

Mom continued. "Your sisters make me crazy sometimes . . . one flying all over the place and the other so delicate." She stood up and with a little laugh, then went on, "But I must say, they keep me young and alert. What a pair!"

She left without another look in my direction. Did she realize, I wondered, tears gathering, what she'd just said? *Hannah, you're steady but dull. Your sisters, however, bring excitement into my life.*

Angrily, I wiped away the tears. *Mom likes me for what I do. Dad loves me for who I am.* Could anything be clearer?

A car honked out in the driveway, and Mom, at the door, called out, "See you Sunday."

I didn't answer, but I didn't need to. She was gone.

After a few minutes I went out to the playhouse to get Paige. She was sitting cross-legged, whispering to the cat and stroking its fur. The cat was definitely pregnant. It looked up at me, and I imagined it saying, "Look what I put up with, just to have a comfortable place to stay."

"Paige," I said, "I think you should leave the cat

alone. If you don't, she may go somewhere else to have her kittens."

"But I'll be her nurse."

"Oh, right. You have such great credentials. Just look at you, you're a regular fur ball. Go in and get cleaned up before Dad gets here."

Paige leaned over the cat and murmured, "Don't worry. I'll be back." The cat closed her eyes.

Paige brushed at her top as we went into the house. I just couldn't understand why her allergies hadn't kicked in. Had she built up an immunity?

While Paige was upstairs changing, Melody drifted into the room, wearing a blue knit top and jeans. "What are the plans for tonight, with Dad?"

"You're going?" I asked, surprised.

"Well, I'm still his daughter. And anyway, I broke a date with Keith for tonight. That'll show him he can't jerk me around."

"Everybody's fighting," I said. "First Mom, then you."

"But my fight with Keith was about his attitude. Mom's was something else."

"Like what?"

"Steve wants to get married, and Mom doesn't."

I was shocked. "Are you kidding?" And then I asked, "Why's Mom against it?"

"I didn't get that part of it. She was talking to her friend Donna on the phone, but when she saw me, she got up and closed the door."

I'd have liked to talk more, but just then Paige came into the room. "I hope we see Lauren again," she said. "She's perfect."

Melody gave me a quick look and then said, "Paige, you need to keep that opinion to yourself."

"Why? She *is* perfect. I wish she were my mother."

Stunned, I blurted, "Paige! What a thing to say!"

Melody chimed in. "Don't say that to Mom or you'll be history. Anyway, how can you like Lauren when you hardly know her? She probably wouldn't be so nice if you had to live with her."

Paige sat on the floor to tie her shoes. "So what? Mom is not nice at all, at least not lately."

"She may just be going through a phase," Melody said. "It'll pass."

I wished I could believe that. It was surprising that Mom didn't want to marry Steve. They got along so well. He had a calming influence on her, and up until now I'd never known them to disagree. She and Dad, on the other hand, had argued a lot.

Dad was getting a fire going in the grill while I brought out the food and utensils. Dad called to Melody, stretched out on a deck chair, to help me, but she couldn't hear a thing because of the earphones.

"It's okay, Dad," I said. "I'd rather do it than get Melody in a bad mood."

"Hannah, you can't give in to her like that," he said, but Paige piped up that she'd help.

When we were ready to eat, Dad made Melody take off the earphones and join us. "No Friday night date?" he asked her.

"I broke up with Keith."

Paige, pounding on the bottom of the ketchup bottle, said, "Mom broke up with Steve, too." The ketchup came out with a blurp, all over the paper plate.

I helped her move the hamburger to a fresh plate. As Paige went off to dispose of the garbage, Dad said to Melody, "Is that so? Your mom and Steve are kaput?"

"Looks like it. Steve wants to get married, and Mom doesn't."

Dad was about to comment when Paige re-appeared, so he changed the subject.

He made Melody do most of the cleaning up, and then I brought out the dessert, a raspberry cheesecake from our favorite bakery.

We hadn't even finished when we heard a car honk out in front and then saw Keith coming around the side of the house. Melody ran to meet him, and they disappeared. She came back a few minutes later and said, "We're going out."

"How did he know you were here?" Dad asked.

"I left a message on the machine. So, see you guys whenever." She rushed over and planted a kiss on Dad's cheek. "Love ya, Pop!"

"Yeah, yeah," he said as she rushed off.

Paige gave a huge sigh and said in Mom's voice, "I just don't know what to do with that girl. First she's mad and then she's not." She became herself again, to ask, "What are we going to do tomorrow?"

"What would you like to do?" Dad asked.

"I'd really like to do something together, as a family." She gave Dad a testing kind of look. "Could Lauren go with us?"

I caught my breath. "Lauren is not family."

Paige said in a sly kind of way, "She could be, Dad, couldn't she? If you married her?"

I expected Dad to say, "I'm not marrying her,"

but he didn't. "I've rented some videos," he said, "in case we want to just hang out this evening. Should we go watch?"

We went into the house, carrying in the dinner things.

Later on that evening, when I went to use the bathroom, I opened the medicine cabinet to get some dental floss. And I saw it . . . right there on the bottom shelf . . . a lipstick. It was an expensive brand, and the shade wasn't anything like those Melody wore. Was it Lauren's lipstick? If so, what was it doing here? And then I saw the toothbrush lying beside it. Dad's toothbrush, and ours, were in the familiar holder on the sink. What did all this mean? I was afraid I knew; Lauren stayed here sometimes.

I had halfway planned, after Paige went to sleep, to sound out Dad about my coming to live with him. But the discovery of Lauren's stuff in the bathroom made me change my mind. Up until now I'd tried to believe that Dad and Lauren were just hanging around together. Dating, sure, but not seriously. I could no longer make myself believe that story.

When we rounded the corner on our way home late Sunday afternoon, Paige said, "I spy Grandma's car in the driveway!" And sounding like Baby Bear discovering Goldilocks, she continued, "And there she is!"

Mom and Grandma were by the front flowerbed, checking out some newly planted mums. When we piled out of the car, Grandma came toward us, hugged Paige and me, and then turned to Dad.

"Richard, it's so good to see you. You look remarkably calm after a weekend with these two."

"I'm on medication, that's why," he joked. "How are you, Elizabeth?"

"Can't complain. You've got some nice mums here—" She caught herself. "Sharon has. Planted them yesterday. I'm quite partial to the bronze ones. They look so *autumn*."

"Very nice," Dad said to Mom. "Well, I'd better be going." He touched Grandma's shoulder. "It was really good to see you."

Pretending to be studying the flowers, Mom said, "You could stay for dinner, Richard."

"Thanks, but I have plans."

To Grandma, Paige whispered, "He's going out with Lauren. She's his girlfriend."

Even with the whisper I heard her, and I think Mom and Dad did, too.

As usual Grandma filled in the gap. "Well, I hope you have a lovely evening, Richard."

He leaned over, kissed her cheek, then told us all good-bye and left.

Paige dashed around to the back yard, and the rest of us went inside. Mom headed for the kitchen, and Grandma sat at the dining room table to talk to me while I set the places.

"How's the quilt coming along, Grandma?" I asked.

"I'm glad to say it's almost finished." She shook out some pills and swallowed them with the iced tea I'd brought out for her. "It's so rewarding to have something you've created yourself," she said.

"I don't think I'd have the patience to make a quilt," I commented, putting out the napkins. Since when had grandma been taking pills?

"Oh, it doesn't have to be a quilt, it can be anything," Grandma continued. "A painting you've done, a birdhouse you've built, a story you've written. The idea is, you've created something that wasn't there before."

Paige came in, and I could tell by her expression that the cat wasn't in the playhouse. She draped an arm around Grandma's shoulder. Grandma patted her hand and kissed it.

"I find it interesting," Grandma said, continuing our conversation, "that it's the cultural things that endure for centuries. When you travel around, what do they show you? Ancient paintings, statues, vases, and jewelry. Those are the things that let us know what life was like in the past."

Paige scooted to sit in a chair. "I'd like to go to Paris and see the Awful Tower."

I laughed, but Grandma said, "Sweetheart, it's called the *Eiffel* Tower. I'm sure you'll see it someday. And when you do, think of your old grandma."

"You're not old," Paige objected, "Just used."

Grandma laughed. "You're right about that."

Mom brought in a platter of chicken, and I helped carry out the rest of the dinner.

As we were eating, Grandma asked, "How's debate?"

"Good. We're arguing about legalizing drugs now."

"As I've said before, I don't think you should be discussing such things," Mom said to me.

"Oh, for heaven's sake, get with it, Sharon," Grandma said. "It's a problem that needs discussion. Drugs aren't going to pack up and go away with that Just Say No nonsense."

"My side opposes making drugs legal," I said.

"Hurray for that, at least," Mom said, never giving in.

Grandma looked at Paige. "And how are you doing?"

"She's doing great," Mom said.

"Not really great," Paige commented. "But I'm doing my best, and that's what counts, isn't it, Mommy?"

"Absolutely."

"Hannah will probably get all A's again," Paige went on. "She always does, so . . . what's the matter, Grandma?"

Grandma was leaning forward, her right hand raised to her forehead.

"Mother—" Mom got up and went to her. "What's wrong?"

Grandma straightened and gave a faint smile. "Just a touch of dizziness I get sometimes. It's all right. It's passed."

Was that what the pills were all about?

"You'd better lie down," Mom said.

"No, no, I'm fine. I'll just go on home and take it easy."

"You can't drive!" Mom protested.

"Of course I can."

"All right. But I'm going to follow you in my car and see that you make it okay. If Richard had stayed," she added in a complaining voice, "he could have driven you."

As they were leaving, Mom turned at the door and said, "Girls, after you've finished eating, clean up, please. I may be a while. I want to see your grandmother settled."

After they'd gone, Paige looked at me with rounded eyes. "Is Grandma going to die?"

Shocked, I said, "Of course not! Don't even say it!"

"Words just pop out. I can't help what I say."

"You can too help what you say. I notice you keep quiet about the cat."

"But she's my special secret!"

I almost went on to tell Paige she should cut the rave remarks about Lauren when Mom was around. But that didn't seem important right now. I had a hunch Mom was really worried about Grandma, and that made me feel worried, too.

twelve

"Hannah! Did you hear me?" Kelsey demanded.

We were in the lunchroom at school. My mind had drifted to Grandma, who insisted she was okay. But I still couldn't help feeling concerned. "What?"

"Why are those kids talking about you?" she asked. "Do you know them?"

I looked. It was a guy named Tim Grossman and Fred somebody. "I don't really know them," I said. They were now looking straight at me. Then Fred elbowed Tim, and Tim got up and walked over to our table.

"Hannah?"

"Yes?"

He sat down at the end of the table. I was next to him. "That's Kelsey," I said, nodding at her, "and Wanda." Lately Wanda had been hanging around us even if, like today, Cheyenne, her new fashion consultant, wasn't around.

"I wanted to ask you something," Tim said.

What was this all about? I hadn't a clue. "Like what?" I asked.

"Your dad's a carpenter, isn't he?"

"Yeah, he is. So?"

"I was wondering . . . You know we're doing a holiday play, don't you?"

"Yes." I'd heard of it.

"Well, I'm head of the stage crew for furniture."

I nodded, although I hadn't known, or cared.

"Some of us built a fireplace . . . a fake one, of course. But it's really pathetic. In fact, it won't even stand up. So I . . . we . . . were wondering if your father—"

"Can you afford him?" Wanda asked. "He doesn't come cheap, you know."

Tim looked flustered. "We don't have any money. We can't pay."

"Then beat it," Wanda said.

I gave her a glance, and Kelsey said, "Keep out of it, Space Ship." Wanda gave her a dirty look.

"I'll talk to my dad," I told Tim. "Maybe he can do it."

The bell rang, meaning lunch hour was over.

We all stood up. "Give me your telephone number, and I'll let you know tonight," I said.

"That's great, thanks," Tim said. "Only I don't have any paper on me."

"Neither do I." I always stashed my stuff in my locker during lunch.

Kelsey said, "Open my backpack. There's a notebook inside."

She turned and I unzipped it. Stuff fell on the floor. Kids who were passing looked and started laughing. "Diapers!" they yelled and punched at each other to look. Everyone was laughing now.

Kelsey's face turned fiery red.

"Chill, you guys!" Wanda shouted. "Haven't you jerks ever seen Pampers before?" She eyed one kid. "You probably wore them through kindergarten!"

I helped Kelsey shove them back into the bag and then picked up the notebook. "What's your number?" I asked.

Tim, looking as if he wished he were somewhere else, mumbled the number and took off.

"Bye, Pampers!" Sally Anderson yelled as she left the room. Other kids picked it up. "Pampers!"

"I'll never live this down," Kelsey said as we finally left. "I wish I'd never been born."

"Take names," Wanda said. "I'll break a few faces for you."

That night I found Tim's number when I started my homework. I dialed Dad and, after telling him about Grandma, I asked if he could build a fireplace.

"I'm sorry, sport, but I just don't have the time right now," he said. "How soon do they need it?"

"Right away."

"Impossible," he said. "But I'll tell you what. Come over to my house. I've got spare lumber lying around. Give me the dimensions and I'll cut it for you, and then you can put it together. There are still a few of my tools down in the basement there."

"I'm not sure I can do it, Dad."

"Of course you can. You've been around enough to know how basic things are built."

"Okay, I'll try."

I called Tim and asked him to get the measurements. "We may be able to do it," I told him.

Right after that, Cheyenne called. "Was it totally awful?" she asked. "When the Pampers fell out of the backpack?"

"That sounds like the name of a movie: *The Day the Diapers Fell out of the Backpack*."

"I wish I'd been there." Cheyenne sighed. "I always miss out on the good stuff. I told Kelsey the best way to handle it."

"How?"

"Laugh along with the kids. That way it will spoil their fun."

Once in a while Cheyenne actually made sense.

I met Dad, as arranged, at his house the next day after school. He checked the dimensions, drew a sketch, and cut the lumber. He even had a piece of molding to trim the inside opening. "When you get the fireplace assembled, use the big staple gun to attach the trim. Then you can cover the staples before you paint it. Or are you going to stain it?"

"Neither. They can do that much themselves. It doesn't have to look perfect, because the audience won't notice. The main thing is for it not to fall over."

Dad laughed. "Well, just don't tell them I made it."

He drove me home with the lumber and my bike in the back of his truck. "How's your grandmother?"

"She's okay. It was a just a dizzy spell, like she said."

That night I started on the fireplace. It went together easily. I didn't realize I'd learned that much about building things just from hanging around Dad.

Suddenly I had the sense that someone else was in the room. I turned and saw Mom. How long had she been watching me?

"So," she said. "I see that you know more about carpentry than you said you did."

"When was that?" And why was I feeling guilty?

"When Steve asked for advice, you acted like little Miss Know-Nothing."

I'd forgotten all about that. "Well . . . Dad reminded me how to do it," I said lamely.

"I see." I expected her to say more, but instead she just went back up the stairs.

Great. Now Mom was ticked at me and Steve would be, too, if she told him. I almost hoped they wouldn't make up.

I worked on the fireplace again the next day after school and then called Tim to say it was almost done. "Do you want it painted or stained?" I asked. I'd decided to do it myself and not let those incompetents mess it up.

"I'll find out," Tim said. "How's Pampers?"

I was a little stunned. "Tim, you'd better stop that—and tell all your friends to stop—unless you want me to hack your fireplace to pieces."

"I was just kidding."

"You heard what I said."

"I heard. It'll stop."

"Fine. Let me know about the finish."

My threat worked. The Pampers joke went away.

"I'm glad I flexed some muscle," Wanda said, taking the credit. I let it go.

When the fireplace was finished, Dad said he'd swing by and pick it up. I hauled it up from the basement and lugged it outside. When Dad saw it, he smiled. He looked at it from all angles, then checked to see how solid it was. "Good work, Hannah," he said. "You're quite the carpenter."

"The paint job could be better," I said. "But it's good enough for on-stage."

We drove it over to the school auditorium, where the kids were rehearsing. When we got there, Dad said, "Go in and tell some of the boys to come out and get it."

I brought out Tim and Fred. Their eyes widened. "Wow, that looks great!" Tim said. "Mr. Pryor, you're one dude carpenter!"

"Well—" Dad started to say.

"Yes, he is," I interrupted. "So long. We've got to leave."

As we drove away, Dad said, "Why didn't you

want to take credit, Hannah? You did a great job."

"I don't want the attention." Mom had made me feel guilty for doing the work, so I just wanted to forget it.

"Sometimes attention is good, if it's deserved."

"Whatever."

"You're a very capable girl. You should be proud of yourself. Not be so modest."

I didn't answer.

"How's everything at home?" Dad asked, noticing my silence.

"Okay." Why should I tell him about Mom's bad mood because of Steve?

"How's debate coming along?"

"Okay." I wondered if Jesse had told about the deal he'd cut with his dad about dropping Space Ship. I was pretty sure he wouldn't convey that little news item to his mother. I wasn't a big fan of Lauren's, but at least I thought she had some principles. As for Dad, he'd blow his stack, even if Jesse wasn't his son. Yet. Would he ever be?

We were at our house now, and I got out of the truck. "Thanks, Dad, for everything. Want to come in?" I was hoping, I don't know, for something crazy. Like maybe he and Mom would talk and set the stage for getting back together. Farfetched, but possible.

"No, thanks, sport," Dad said. "I have to run over to a new site we're looking at. I'm a little late as it is."

"Well, thanks for helping with the fireplace." I leaned over and kissed his cheek and then he took off.

Mom wasn't home, but she'd left a note, saying she'd gone over to the trucking office. I was just putting down the paper when Paige came running in, gasping.

"Hannah, come out right away! She's having it!"

"What?"

"Butterfly! She's having her kitten!" Paige was breathing heavily. "Come right away!"

"Paige." I took hold of her arm. "Now, calm down."

"No! Come outside with me!"

She raced out and I followed. I have to admit I was a little excited myself.

When we got to the playhouse, Butterfly looked up and gave us a glance before going back to lick a soggy little white creature.

"Oh, look! It's real! It's a baby kitten!"

And then Butterfly stopped licking, made little sounds, and bingo! There was another kitten, wrapped in a film. The cat bit it off so that the new yellow bundle, really wet-looking, was freed.

Paige was now on her hands and knees, her face not far from the kittens. And then she started to gasp.

"Paige, get back. You're going to frighten them." Then I was frightened myself as my sister began wheezing. I'd witnessed her asthma attacks before and knew this was going to be a bad one. "Come into the house," I said, taking her arm.

She pulled back and shook off my hand. "Leave me alone!"

"Paige, you've got to—"

Then she turned her face up to me, and I could see even she knew she was in trouble now. "I . . . I . . ."

I picked her up and carried her into the house. Her gasps were like rattles. Where was her medication? I put her down on the sofa, ran to the bathroom, and scrabbled around in the medicine cabinet. I found the pills, but would they kick in soon enough? Usually it took ten minutes or so, and I wasn't sure that we had that kind of time.

I rushed back and handed Paige the pills. Gasping, she pushed my hand away. "Can't swallow." I gave her the inhalator, hoping it would buy some time. She was taking huge breaths when I left to phone Mom.

There was only a recorded message, the kind that said, "If you're calling about . . ." I didn't have time for that. I slammed down the phone and was about to call Dad when I remembered he was out of reach. The truck didn't have a phone. I called Jesse's number. Thank goodness Lauren, not the machine, picked up.

"Lauren," I gasped, "it's Hannah. I need your help. Mom's not here—and Dad's—it's Paige! She can't breathe, with her asthma! I'm so scared! I don't know what to do!"

"Hang up, Hannah. I'll call the paramedics, then I'll drive right over. Now, try your best to calm Paige."

She arrived just as the paramedics came, siren screaming. They were carrying Paige out on a stretcher when Mom pulled into the driveway. "What's going on?" she called out.

"Paige is having a really bad attack!" I said, sobbing.

Then Mom spied Lauren. "What are you doing here?" she asked, her voice hardening.

"Hannah couldn't find you, or her father, so she called me."

"Oh, wonderful. First you took over my husband, and now you're taking over my daughter!"

"I'm . . . sorry . . . but . . ." Lauren was at a loss.

"Mom, stop that!" I said through my sobs. "She's the one who called the paramedics . . . you should be grateful!"

"I'm—" Mom cut short whatever she was about to say because they'd put Paige in the ambulance and were about to close the doors. Mom rushed over. "Hold on! I'm riding with you!"

"Can I go, too?" I asked, following her.

"No, you stay here. I'll call."

She got inside and they took off, siren at full screech.

I went back to Lauren, who was standing there looking hurt.

"I'm so sorry," I said, "about what Mom said . . . She doesn't—"

"Shh," she said, holding me close. "Your mother was upset, as she had every right to be. I mean, that child . . ." She smoothed my hair as I continued to sob against her.

"Do you think Paige will be all right?" Of course, I knew that no one, especially Lauren, who'd never witnessed one of these attacks, could say. I just wanted assurance.

"They'll know what to do at the hospital," Lauren said. "In fact, they'll be treating her on the ride there. The paramedics are trained for emergencies, you know."

"I know." I pulled away and wiped the tears from my face.

"Is your sister home, Hannah?"

"Melody? No. She never is."

"Do you want to come back to your father's house with me? I'll try to locate him."

"No, I'd better stay here and wait for Mom's call. I'll be all right."

"I hate to leave you here alone, but . . . it's better if I leave."

I knew what she was thinking. Mom wouldn't like it if Lauren made herself at home in our house. "Really, it's okay."

"All right, then." She leaned over and kissed the top of my head. "You're a brave, wonderful girl, Hannah. I wish I had a daughter just like you."

Melody came home soon after Lauren left. I told her what had happened, including Mom's reaction. Melody said, "Oh, man, I'm glad I wasn't witness to that little scene."

A while later Dad called for news, and when I said there wasn't any, he told me he'd go to the hospital. I'd just hung up when Mom called.

"She's all right, but it was a close call," she said. "I'm glad the paramedics got there when they did." I wondered if Mom remembered it was

Lauren who'd called them, and if she was at least a little ashamed of the things she'd said.

Paige recovered quickly and was able to come home the next day, looking none the worse for her experience. She'd confessed to Mom about the cat, and the three of us went out to the playhouse to check on her.

"Now, stand back" Mom said to my sister. "We don't need a repeat of what happened yesterday."

There were now three kittens, one yellow, one white, and one yellow and white, nursing and kneading their paws against their mother while Butterfly purred with contentment.

"Paige, you should have told me," Mom said, smiling in spite of herself as she gazed at the cat family. "But I have to say they're awfully cute."

"I guess we'll have to hang on to all of them," Paige said, hope in her voice.

"I guess we'll have to hang on to just one," Mom said. "And it will have to stay outside. And you're not to cuddle it close to your face."

"It wasn't the cat—it was the excitement that made me wheeze," Paige said.

"Even so," Mom said.

I was a little surprised that she had given in so

easily, but as we all knew, Paige could get an attack just from being angry and frustrated.

"And now, young lady, you're going into the house and into bed," Mom said. "And don't even think of sneaking out to see the cats tonight."

As a backup I added, "If you make a pest of yourself, Paige, the mother cat will move the kittens, and you may never see them again."

"That's right," Mom agreed, as if she knew.

Paige was asleep when Dad called later that evening.

From the living room sofa I could hear Mom in the kitchen, telling him that Paige was fine now.

I couldn't hear everything Mom said. In fact, I wasn't paying that much attention, but I did pick up at the words, "Please tell her . . . Lauren . . . that I'm sorry I flared up at her yesterday. As you might imagine, I was quite upset, seeing the ambulance and then her."

Dad must have reassured Mom because she said, "Well, I just wanted her to know I didn't mean it. I was just frantic with worry."

When she came back into the room and sat down by me, I pretended to be fascinated by the weather report on TV.

"What do you think of her?" Mom asked, eyes

on the reporter, who was doing his boring routine with the highs and lows.

"Who? Lauren?" I cleared my throat. "She's okay."

"No, really."

"Mom, she's very nice. Friendly. But she doesn't try to . . . like . . . take over."

"That's good." A little huskiness came into Mom's voice. "I guess I'm selfish, but I want to keep my girls for myself."

"Mom, don't worry." I put my arm around her and she laid her head on my shoulder. "We'll always be your girls."

"I know that," she said, her voice muffled. "I know that."

thirteen

"I'm going to a really great party," Melody confided in me one night. She had actually come into my room. "But don't tell Mom."

"I report every word you say to her, you know that."

My sister half-smiled, knowing I was being sarcastic. "It's coming up next week. Do we have a Polaroid? Seems to me like we used to have one."

"It's probably in the hall closet. Why? Do you need it for the party?"

"It's going to be a photo scavenger hunt. Cool, huh?"

"I don't get it."

"You know what a scavenger hunt is, don't you?"

"Where you get a list of weird objects that you have to find in a given time?"

"Right. But this goes beyond. They'll give us a list of strange places where we have to take photos. We go in groups, in cars, and time means everything. Along with imagination."

"Who's driving?"

"Who's driving? Is that all you can say? Kids with licenses, of course. And cars."

I wasn't surprised. Half of Melody's crowd is older than she is. "When?"

"A week from Saturday." She looked around. "This room is so antiseptic. You could perform surgery in here."

"I like it that way."

"You would." She left.

I hated it when Melody told me she was planning to do something that was a little risky, like driving around wildly, and then asked me not to tell Mom. It made me feel like a conspirator. I didn't care how many parties or what kind she went to. I just didn't want to get caught in the middle.

The thought of going to debate was beginning to be like the thought of going to the dentist.

Melody calls ours the fang-yanker. Well, I felt that I was being yanked around by debate, and it was a pain, too, in its own way.

Even Jesse looked a bit concerned as we were gathering in the debate room. "I have the feeling," he said to me, "that there's something shady going on."

"You should know all about that," I told him. "Shady deals, I mean."

"Still tweaked about Space Ship? She got over it. So should you."

"In case the word hasn't gotten to you, she wants to be called Wanda now."

"Yeah, okay." The others on our team had slowly drifted over to us. "All set?" Jesse asked. "I hope you've all memorized the arguments that I printed out for you. Everything's there in black and white, bing, bing, bing."

"Right!" we all agreed.

Jesse smiled, pleased with our response. "They go first, so we do the rebuttal, and that's when we really kick them." He looked around the group. "You all have the program, know what you're supposed to say?"

"Somewhere." Jennifer grubbed in her backpack. "Here it is." She glanced at her assignment. "I talk about how if drugs were legalized innocent kids could get high just from eating pot brownies. Good point."

"You got it," Jesse said. "Be strong, confident in your approach."

Mrs. Waltermire clapped her hands and said, "Ready, everybody? Let's begin."

Katie, from the other side, got up and started speaking. It was a little general until she said, "And if kids could get high just from eating pot-laced brownies, I say, 'All you need do is just be careful what you eat.' If you suspect someone's mother is into drugs, don't go to that kid's house and eat brownies. I mean, you have to show a little judgment."

I think all of our mouths dropped open. Under his breath, Jesse said, "I don't believe this."

"What'll I say? What'll I say?" Jennifer asked, panicking.

"Just talk," Jesse said. "Say anything."

The other team sat with folded arms, smiling.

"I believe . . . uh . . . I don't think you should eat brownies anyway," Jennifer stumbled. "They're fattening." And then she sat down.

Jesse groaned. The other team laughed. I felt shaken. What was going on here, anyway?

Larry then stood up for the opposition. "Colleagues, let me just say that drugs are not the problem. People are the problem. People always want what is forbidden. So don't forbid drugs. Let people buy them and get bored." He cleared his throat. "Now, if you say . . ."

Here it comes, I thought. I already sensed what Larry was going to say next.

"If you say, 'Well, cigarettes are illegal for kids, but still they light up—'" Jesse and I now said the rest of the sentence from memory. "How far would they go if cigarettes weren't forbidden? They'd smoke like stoves, openly and often."

I felt numb, and I suspect our whole team felt the same as Larry continued, "But my answer to that is, it's the duty of school and home to put a stop to kids smoking. Keep the law out of it. Let the cops spend their time collaring crooks."

"I just don't believe this," Jesse gasped. "Go, Roy, if you can."

Roy, whose argument had been totally nuked, stumbled to his feet and said, "Yeah, that's what they ought to do. Go with it!" He shot his arm in the air like an Olympics gold medal winner and sat down.

"Idiot," Jesse mumbled. "You agreed with him."

Mrs. Waltermire looked flustered. She knew

this wasn't going right but didn't have a clue what had happened. Our team had fallen apart.

"Time out?" Jesse asked.

The teacher nodded. "Two minutes." I don't know if this was regulation or not, but she allowed it.

Our team huddled. "Clearly," Jesse said, "they've got a copy of our strategy. How they got it, I don't know."

I happened to glance at Wanda and saw the sly smile on her face. I knew then that she was the traitor.

"Hannah," Jesse said to me, "you're our last speaker, and our last hope. What can you say?"

"I'll think of something." I didn't know what it could be, but I had to give the other side a fight. My choice would have been to go over and smack that smug smile off Brandon's face, but I'd have to do it with words. If that was possible.

"Time's up," called Mrs. Waltermire.

We sat and listened to what we knew the other team would say. Linda said it. "If drugs were legalized, we wouldn't have teens running away from home and having drugs supplied to them by lowlifes, and then being forced into robbery and prostitution. They could get their drugs legally and stay with their parents." She frowned a bit, trying to remember and then went on.

"And if you say—" I could feel our whole team bracing themselves for the words they knew would follow. "If you say that legalizing drugs would make kids even wilder and crazier than they are now, well . . ." She looked blank, obviously forgetting what came next. "Well, you're just wrong," she said, and sat down.

"Go, Hannah," Jesse said. "Hit 'em."

I stood up. The nervousness I might have felt had given way to anger. "Thank you for letting me reply to that," I said. I noticed Brandon nudging his neighbor.

"You have stated that children shouldn't be allowed to go to homes where the mother—or father—could pass around drug-laced brownies. Wonderful. And who's going to determine just which parents those are? Should parents make other parents sign papers stating that theirs is a drug-free home? Or maybe make parents wear wires?" It sounded good even if it made no sense.

I noticed the other team had stopped smiling.

"And who is going to monitor the stores? If a child goes to buy a candy bar, might he or she also buy nose candy?"

I could hear my team's murmurs of approval.

"And if kids could buy drugs on any street corner without fear of arrest, perhaps they wouldn't run away from home. Instead, they'd be locked up in a drug abuse center."

Brandon was glaring at me and muttering to his friends. I knew he was ticked because my arguments hadn't appeared on our outline. I was making them up as I went along.

"Guns kill and shouldn't be left around where kids can get at them. Drugs also kill. Legalized drugs could be anywhere in the house, within reach of toddlers, or even brought in by the baby sitter. Do we want this? I say no! We cannot make something so deadly as drugs legal . . . and ruin, or even end, innocent young lives!"

My team applauded as I sat down. The opposition looked stunned.

"Well," Mrs. Waltermire took over. "That concludes the debate. And while your team—" she looked at Brandon—"made some persuasive arguments, I would say that Jesse's team came through with a stunning rebuttal. I therefore announce his side the winner."

We all raised our palms in the up on the roof gesture.

As we meandered out to the hall, Brandon

blurted out, "Your team cheated. You didn't stick to the schedule."

"Oh?" Jesse raised his eyebrows. "And what schedule was that? The one you stole from one of our members?"

"We didn't steal it, we—" Brandon stopped, caught by his own words. He fumbled on. "Anyway, who cares? It was just a stupid debate."

"With some pretty stupid people," our Jennifer said.

"Waltermire wanted your team to win because she's against drugs herself," Brandon muttered as he took off.

Cheyenne joined us as the others on her team left. "Wanda," she said, "I know you're grateful for my help, fashion-wise. And you're so welcome. But you guys didn't need to go beyond, to make our team win."

"You didn't win," Jennifer pointed out. "We did."

"Oh?" Cheyenne glanced around. "I must have missed that part."

Jesse now eyed Wanda. "So this is what you meant by that message you left on my machine. You said I'd be sorry. That was a low-down thing you did, but it all turned out well for me anyway."

"Go soak your head in seaweed" were Wanda's parting words as she stalked off.

Jesse laughed, then turned to us. "Team, we did it. Congratulations all around!"

As we left, I hardly heard Cheyenne's chatter. I was wondering how Jesse had won at home. He must have negotiated with his father for something good. Well, what did I care? But I felt really betrayed by Wanda. She'd put up our team for grabs just to get back at Jesse.

Still, we'd won. I knew it was my final argument that had clinched it. The best part was that it had come entirely from me, not Jesse. I'd done it myself, and on the spur of the moment.

No one else had acknowledge that fact, but I didn't mind. It was enough for me to realize I was a fighter, someone who came through in a crisis.

That night Jesse called me. "I . . . uh . . . didn't want the others to feel left out, so I didn't thank you properly for saving the debate. I want you to know I appreciate it, though."

Annoyed by his smug tone, I couldn't help saying, "This may come as a shock, Jesse, but I didn't do it for your sake. Do you think everything's about you?"

There was silence, and I could almost see him blushing. "I'm sorry," he said. "It's just that winning meant so much to me. Didn't it to you?"

"Of course I wanted to win. But my big goal was to shoot down their team. Especially after that betrayal by Wanda."

After another pause, Jesse said, "In her own twisted little way, she thought she was justified. Maybe she was."

"What is this I'm hearing, Jesse? You're admitting you're a lowlife wheeler-dealer?"

"I wouldn't say that," he said. "It's the way of the world. Ask my dad."

"Speaking of your father, what was the deal you made with him for getting rid of Wanda? What do you get?"

"A trip to Hawaii."

For a moment I was stunned. "You're kidding."

"Nope. We're going over the Christmas holidays."

I just couldn't believe this.

"Hannah? You still there?"

I found my voice. "Have you told your mother? Not about the trip to Hawaii, but how you made it happen?"

"Not yet. Dad'll tell her. Maybe not about the

Wanda part. That's not important. You won't tell her, will you?"

"Of course not. You will."

"I will?" For the first time he sounded like a little boy. "But what if she won't let me go to Hawaii?"

"Tough. You'll go some time when you deserve it."

I heard Jesse sigh. At last he said, "Okay, I'll do it. You've made me feel guilty."

I felt like saying, "It's about time someone did," but that would be a slam against his mother. She should take lessons from my mom.

Then Jesse said in a tone I'd never heard before, "Hannah, I have to say, you're a good person. Like your father."

What a breakthrough remark! Could it mean that Jesse had taken the first step toward becoming an actual human? I hoped so, though I had my doubts.

I was more than surprised later that night when my dad phoned to congratulate me for winning the debate. "Jesse said your team would've lost if it hadn't been for you."

"Jesse said that?"

"He actually said that."

"Wow. Hard to believe."

Dad laughed. "He's really not a bad kid when you get to know him."

"Uh-huh." I wondered if Jesse was just oiling up Dad in advance, for when he heard about the Hawaiian caper. I wouldn't put it past him. But I couldn't totally blame Jesse for the way he worked people. He'd learned it from his father. I was lucky. In my case, I had a father who tried to teach me how to be a decent human being.

fourteen

At school everyone knew about the preholiday play that was coming up soon. How could they not? Almost every day along with routine announcements came the message "May we remind you that tickets are going fast [in their dreams!] for the great upcoming play *Sister Sally's Dreamwagon*. We urge you to get your tickets now. And bring your parents. This is a family play."

"*Family play*," Wanda said at lunch one day. "That'll kill all interest."

"So you're not going to see it?" Kelsey asked.

Wanda, for once, looked ill at ease. In a small voice she said, "I don't have anyone to go with. My parents would laugh their heads off if I even suggested it."

"Come with us, then," I said, as my friends gave me the Look. I didn't care. Even after what she'd done, I had to feel a little sorry for Wanda.

Later Kelsey said to me in the hall, "Why did you have to invite her? She's like a barnacle as it is, always hanging on to us."

"Come on, she's trying to fit in. You said yourself that she looks approximately normal since Cheyenne worked her magic. And besides that, we're the only kids in school she can count on to be civil to her."

"Did you ever find out," Kelsey asked, opening her locker to toss in a book, "what actually happened with her and Jesse? They're like strangers in the mist."

"Oh, you know how it goes," I said evasively. "Who's coming to the play from your family?"

"Just me. Cheyenne's going to meet me there. How about your folks?"

"Dad wants to go. I guess he feels he has a stake in the play because of the fireplace. I built it, but he gave me the materials."

Kelsey had no sooner left than Jesse appeared. He acted as if he'd been waiting for her to take off.

"Just wanted to update you on the Hawaiian

trip," he said. "It looks like I may be going after all."

I eyed him. "Then you didn't tell your mother?" I might have known.

"I told you I would, and I did."

I felt a little disappointed in Lauren. Didn't she care?

"She was bent out of shape at first, but then she laid down some conditions."

"Oh?"

"Get this. She cut the cleaning woman to every other week and said that I had to keep the house up to an acceptable level the week in between."

"I do that all the time," I said. "We don't have a cleaning woman."

"Wow. What a concept." Jesse shook his head. "So here I am, vacuuming, dusting, picking up stuff, taking out the garbage—"

"I know the drill," I interrupted.

"And you know what? It's actually rather satisfying, seeing the results."

I was thinking that I'd never experienced that particular thrill, but then, cleaning was old hat to me.

"Did your dad tell you that he taught me how to rewire a lamp?" he went on. "We were going to toss it out. Imagine. And it was so easy to repair!"

This, too, was no news flash. Dad had taught me years ago.

"And just last week I learned another cool thing. Mom had lost a ring down the sink drain, and was feeling bad, because although it wasn't a great ring, it was one her mother had given her. Your father showed me how to open the pipes. And sure enough, the ring was in that curvy part—"

"The trap?"

"Yeah, the trap." Jesse looked pleased. Maybe there was some hope for him after all. And then I thought, with a little pang, there would be if he spent enough time with my father.

Jesse went on, "Next he's going to show me how to change a flat tire."

"I can't believe," I told him, "that you don't already know how. It's fairly common knowledge."

Far from being insulted, Jesse only replied, "Not in our family. We've always just called Triple-A to come take care of it."

Cheyenne was approaching, so we cut the conversation.

I was glad to know that Jesse's little bribery

business had hit the skids, and that he was finally finding out how real people actually worked for what they wanted. But I had to admit I felt a little jealous at the closeness developing between Dad and his girlfriend's kid. He was teaching Jesse the same kinds of things he'd always taught me. Was I being replaced?

The night of the play Dad picked up Paige and me and also Cheyenne, Kelsey, and Wanda. "I feel like the coach of a girls' basketball team," he said.

"That'll be the day," Wanda muttered.

Our seats were the first six in about the fifteenth row, with Dad sitting on the aisle and then me, then Paige, then Cheyenne, then Wanda, and Kelsey.

"How's the cat family?" Cheyenne asked Paige. "I hear those kittens made you sick."

"It wasn't the cats," Paige said. "The allergist gave me tests, and I'm not allergic to fur after all. It was the excitement that did it, he said. I'm supposed to stay calm whenever possible."

In other words, we have to let her have her own way, I'd thought when she first told us.

"Can I have one of the kittens?" Cheyenne asked.

Paige caught her breath. "You'd take one?"

"Sure, maybe even two, to keep each other company. Mouser has become a real drag. All he does now is eat and sleep."

"I won't mind giving them up so much if I know I can come to your house to visit them," Paige said. "Their names are Snowball, Butterscotch, and Marmalade. Which two do you want?"

"You decide."

I didn't hear Paige's answer because I happened to notice Dad looking at someone. It was Lauren and Jesse, across the aisle and a few rows ahead of us. Even without Jesse, I'd have recognized Lauren from the back, because of her long stream of dark hair.

"Excuse me," Dad said, getting up and going to them. In just a few minutes he'd taken Jesse's seat and Jesse had come back and sat next to me.

"Love's young dream," he murmured. He smiled and said hi to all the girls and even kept his smile when Wanda gave him the finger. "I can't fault her attitude," he said to me, "but isn't she better off, really, having you great guys to hang with?"

The lights dimmed, and the curtains opened. I hardly heard the first bits of dialogue because my attention was focused on the fireplace. It looked great. Actually, maybe too great, because it made the rest of the furnishings look pretty pathetic.

At the intermission, Jennifer, from my debate team, came up with a group of her friends. "Did you really do it?" she asked.

"Do what?"

"Didn't you read the program? Look." She pointed to a paragraph of acknowledgments. It said, "Fireplace by Hannah Pryor."

"You've got all kinds of talents!" she said, while her friends nodded agreement.

"It's just something I learned from my father," I said. "No big deal."

As they walked away, Jesse looked at me with a respect he'd never shown before. "You really are good," he said. And then added, "For a girl." Kelsey made a fist toward his face, and he laughed.

"I wonder," I said to Kelsey, "how they found out I built the fireplace and not Dad?"

"I told them. Because you're too modest," she said.

The rest of the play was something of a blur

to me, I was in such a glow. I remembered what Grandma had said that time, about the great feeling you get when you do something creative. The fireplace would never find a place in a museum or anything like that, but what was important was the fact that I'd made it. I was the one who'd put it up there for everyone to see.

That evening, which had been such a high, ended on a very low note. Melody met Paige and me at the door. She'd been crying, and her mascara had left blue streaks on her cheeks. "Grandma's in the hospital," she said.

"What? What happened?" I could feel my heart thump.

"They think it's a stroke. Mom's been there for a couple of hours. She told me to call Aunt Helen in Phoenix, to let her know, and she's flying in tomorrow."

Paige, now crying, asked, "Is Grandma going to die?"

Melody flicked a look at me before saying, "No, nothing like that. She's just very sick."

"What exactly is a stroke?" I wanted to know.

"Search me," Melody said. "Something to do with being paralyzed. For a while, anyway. Most people come out of it just fine." She didn't look or sound very convincing.

There was nothing we could do except wait for word from the hospital. Melody sent Paige to bed around midnight. Mom's call came a little while afterward.

"She's stabilized and asleep. I'm going to stay through the night. Are you girls all right there?"

"Sure," Melody said. "I've sent Paige to bed and Hannah's on her way." Turning her back on my look of indignation, she said, "Was it a serious stroke?" And then, "Well, that's good. Aunt Helen will be here tomorrow." After another pause she said, "No, nobody's called him. Isn't it kind of late now? To spring the news on Dad?" And then she said, "Yeah, that's a good idea."

After Melody hung up, she told me Mom would let Dad know in the morning. He'd always been fond of Grandma. And Mom had also said that we should go to school as usual and that she'd pick up Aunt Helen at the airport.

When we got home the next day—the longest day of my life—Mom and Aunt Helen were sitting in the living room drinking coffee.

Aunt Helen is two years younger than Mom, but you'd think she was the older one, she's such a know-it-all. Her hair is cut short, and her skin is quite tanned and wrinkled from her being out on the golf course so much. She gripped each of us in a vise-like hug and made the usual comments about how much we'd all grown.

Melody, who wants to keep her petite, baby-doll status, said, "I've already reached my full height."

"Good," Aunt Helen retorted. "So that frees you to work on mental and emotional growth." She said it innocently enough, but I could tell from Mom's startled look that she'd already filled in her sister about Melody's recent behavior.

"How's Grandma?" I asked.

"She's doing well," Mom said. "They've moved her out of intensive care. She wants to go home, but they're going to keep her in the hospital for a few more days."

"Have you girls heard from lover boy?" Aunt Helen asked. Ignoring Mom's frown, she went on, "Did he bother to call?" My aunt couldn't resist getting in a little dig at Dad because in her wrong-headed way she'd always blamed him for the divorce.

"If you mean my father," Melody said, still burned about the maturity remark, "yes, I called. He said to convey his best wishes."

"Huh," Aunt Helen said. "How generous of him."

We had an early dinner so Mom and Aunt Helen could get back to the hospital in time for visitors' hour.

"I'm depending on all of you to stay home this evening in case we need to get in touch with you," Mom said as they were leaving. She didn't look at Melody, but we all knew who she meant.

"We'll be here," I said for all or us.

"Who does Aunt Helen think she is?" Melody muttered. "Miss Manners? No one asked for her advice."

As soon as we heard the car pull out, Paige said, "I think I'll go spend some time with my cats." She came back about fifteen minutes later, carrying the yellow and white kitten, the one she was going to keep. "I want Marmalade to get used to the house, where he's going to live when it gets freezing outside," she said.

"You hope," Melody said under her breath. We all played with the kitten, who seemed to like these new surroundings, with so many things to explore. Then we all took turns holding and petting it. Even Melody talked baby-kitty talk to it.

By the next day Grandma was doing much better. On Friday Aunt Helen went to the hospital while Mom stayed home to get caught up on her work. Then that night it was Mom's turn. She took Melody and Paige with her.

I knew why Melody wanted to go this particular evening. It was so she'd be free tomorrow night for the Polaroid party she was so excited about.

She'd told me earlier, "I got some scoop from Kristi, who made me promise not to tell anyone, but I can tell you. One of the things we have to shoot is a theater marquee with a one-word movie listed. Like *Armageddon*. And to prove we were there, we have to take a photo of all of us standing underneath it."

"Who'll take the picture if all of you have to be in it?"

"Oh, anyone. Another is all of us behind the counter of a fast-food place. It'll be a blast. Oh, and another is in a cemetery."

"That sounds creepy. At night."

"Doesn't it? I can hardly wait. Don't tell Mom," she added as a matter of course.

"You found the camera?"

"Yeah, in the hall closet. But we don't need it. Keith has one."

"How do you know he'll be on your team?"

"We'll arrange it."

Knowing my sister, she'd manage to do it.

The next night a car honked in the driveway and in a flash Melody was out of there.

"Where's she off to now?" Aunt Helen asked me. Mom was in her room, getting ready to go to the hospital. I was all set to go with her.

Paige butted in. "Melody is always off somewhere. She just nearly drives me over the edge." In Mom's voice, of course.

I was so used to this line that it hardly registered, but Aunt Helen reacted like a shot.

"It's not nice to mimic other people, Paige," she snapped.

My sister looked truly confused. Up to now everyone had always thought it was cute.

"How old are you?" Aunt Helen went on.

"Eight," Paige almost whispered.

"Eight? Then stop acting like a five-year-old. I know everyone around here babies you, but—"

"I *am* the baby," Paige said.

"Baby of the family, maybe, but that doesn't mean you need to go on—" She stopped as Mom came into the room.

"Ready?" she asked. I got up.

Paige ran to Mom and wrapped her arms around her waist. "I want to go with you," she begged.

"But you were there last night," Mom said. "It's Hannah's turn."

"But can't I go, too?" Her voice quivered.

"See, Paige, that's what I was telling you," Aunt Helen said. And to Mom, "Don't give in to her. Just go."

Reluctantly, under my aunt's steady gaze, Mom unwrapped Paige's arms. "Calm down," she said.

I caught my breath. Would Paige carry on until she had an asthma attack? "She could go with us, couldn't she?" I was buckling under, knowing it wasn't right and yet feeling afraid. "There were two girls last night, and the nurses didn't care," I pointed out.

"Sharon . . ." Aunt Helen warned, letting me know they'd already discussed Paige (along with Melody).

"Stay here," Mom said to Paige more firmly. "No more whining."

We left in spite of Paige's full-blown tears. As we were driving, I said, "I feel bad for Paige. I hope she doesn't get too upset."

"Hannah, we can't let your sister hold us

hostage with threats of getting sick. She's got to learn how to cope with life's little disappointments. It's all a part of growing up."

That was Aunt Helen talking, not my mother. I wondered what great things my aunt had had to say about me.

fifteen

Grandma, sitting up in the hospital bed, smiled when she saw us. I noticed her smile was a little lopsided. "Hannah, sweetheart," she greeted me. It came out a bit like *Hannah, sweetar.*

"Hi, Grandma," I said, leaning over to kiss her cheek. "How's it going?"

"Awwite." I pretended not to notice her slurred speech.

Mom kissed her, too, and Grandma didn't have to say too much after that, with Mom keeping up a running commentary. She talked about her job and told a story about Aunt Helen totally rearranging our kitchen cupboards when no one was around.

Grandma gave her crooked smile and a little dismissive wave of her hand, meaning, I guess, that that was just like Aunt Helen.

"Of course, I'll move everything back the way it was after she leaves," Mom went on.

"How's school?" Grandma then asked me.

"School? It's fine. You know that fireplace I told you about on the phone?" Grandma nodded. "Well, it turned out pretty well."

"Pretty well?" Mom interrupted. "I heard it was the best part of the play, including the acting."

"Oh, come on, Mom," I said. "It wasn't that spectacular."

"And what about debate?" Grandma asked me. It sounded like "debay."

"Pretty boring. Some of the kids on the other team wanted to drop out after they lost the one about drugs, but Mrs. Waltermire wouldn't let them." I paused. "Jesse says that he's beginning to think the whole team, not just Cheyenne, are ABCOMs."

I understood Grandma's next words even though they were slurred. "What does ABCOM mean?"

"It means 'A Bad Case of Moonburn.' You know—loony." I sighed. "Sometimes I think everyone's moonburned but me. The reason I'm not is I'm just too ordinary."

"Ordinary? Never!" Grandma fixed me with a look and struggled through what she was about to say. "Hannah, you are the most remarkable girl I know."

"Really?"

"Most definitely." With a glance at Mom, she mumbled something that was clear to both of us. "Your sisters could use some of your good sense."

Mom didn't have a chance to reply because just then Dad came into the room.

"Hi, everyone," he said. "I know it's late, Elizabeth, but I just wanted to stop by to see how you're doing."

"I doee fine," she said. She looked really pleased. Sometimes I think she feels closer to Dad than to her own daughter. "I'm gooee home soon now."

"If you follow the doctor's orders," Mom said.

Grandma shrugged, then turned back to Dad. "Don't you hab the girls this weekend?" she asked.

Mom answered for him. "Helen wanted to spend some time with the girls while she's here."

So she can find fault and try to shape us up, I thought.

"How is Helen?" Dad asked Mom.

"The same as always," she said.

A little amused expression passed over my father's face. He had to know that my aunt was no fan of his.

After a little more conversation, a nurse popped into the room. "Is there a Hannah Pryor here?"

Amazed, I said, "I'm Hannah."

"There's a phone call for you out at the nurse's station. I'll show you where."

Everyone looked a little baffled, which is how I felt as I followed her out of the room. Why the nurse's station? If one of my friends had been told by Aunt Helen where I was, why didn't they just ring Grandma's room?

"Try to make it brief," the nurse said, as she set the phone up on the counter for me.

"Hey, Hannah," the voice said. It was Melody.

"Why are you calling me here instead of in Grandma's room?"

"Top secret. You have to do something for me."

That was my sister. Not *will you?* but *you have to.*

"What?"

"We just ran out of film. Stupid Keith didn't bring an extra, and we don't have time to find an open store to get another pack." The excitement in her voice made her words come out in a rush. "I know the camera at home has film in it, so go get it and bring it out to Ridgemont Cemetery. We'll be there soon."

"Melody!" I protested. "Why can't *you* do it?"

"It's too far from where we are. Hannah, just do it!" She was all but screaming. "Now!"

"Okay," I heard myself saying.

What did I just do? Why did I agree? I asked myself on the way back to the room. "I've got to leave," I said.

"Don't be silly," Mom said. "We're not going to shorten our visit with your grandmother just because of your friends."

Dad must have noticed my panic because he said, "I've got to get going myself. Just wanted to stop by and check out my favorite relative." He leaned over and kissed Grandma's cheek. "Come on, Hannah," he said, "I'll drop you off."

In the elevator Dad said, "You're so tense. What's going on?"

I told him about Melody's game and what she'd asked—or rather told—me to do.

"And how does she expect you to get to the cemetery?"

I hadn't thought of that. "Take a cab, I guess."

"Oh, great," Dad said, exasperated. "No, I'll drive you. But I'm going to have a few words with Melody."

"She's just caught up in the game, Dad." I felt better, having Dad with me. As we drove home, I told him that for the contest they had to take photos in lots of places, including the cemetery.

Dad picked up the car phone and called Lauren. "I'll be back a little late," he told her. "I have an errand to run with Hannah. I'll explain later."

At home, relieved to see that Aunt Helen wasn't downstairs, I grabbed the camera and dashed back to Dad's car.

The cemetery in question was close to our suburb. Dad knew how to get there, so it didn't take long. Just before we turned up the entrance drive, Keith and his crew roared in ahead of us.

Melody leaped out of the car and rushed over to ours. "Hi, Dad, where's the camera?" she called out, too excited, I guess, to wonder why Dad had shown up.

I reached past Dad and held the camera out for her.

She waved it in the air, and her team swarmed around the gate that bore the name of the cemetery. Then she yelled for me to come take the photo.

I ran over, caught up in the excitement myself, and shot the picture. Without so much as a thank-you, they all dashed back to Keith's car. They had swung around and were heading out when another car came racing in. The two vehicles were aimed straight at each other but then Keith swerved, and his car rammed into a tree.

There was a horrible sound of metal being crushed and glass breaking. I sat, stunned, but

Dad leaped out and ran to the smashed car. I couldn't move. Could this really have happened, so suddenly? What about my sister?

By the time my legs worked enough for me to get over to the car, Keith was climbing out, bloody but alive, and the two in the back also staggered out. But what about Melody?

I felt removed, as though I were watching a scene in a movie. Melody was still inside. Was she dead? Dad yanked open the door and leaned in to check. "Oh, my God," he said. From behind him, I saw my sister with blood streaming down her face. She must be dead. But no—no, she wasn't.

"My leg!" she screamed. "I can't move my leg!"

Dad turned to me. "Call 911 on the car phone."

I couldn't. I couldn't.

One of the boys from the other car said, "I'll do it," and ran to Dad's car. The others were all huddled around Dad, as he tried to calm Melody while blotting her bloody face with a handkerchief. *My sister's blood.* I felt weak. *How can all that blood be coming out of my sister?*

It seemed like an eternity, but I was told later that it was only ten minutes until the paramedics and police arrived. As they rushed to my sister, I stood at a little distance, sobbing and shaking. Was her leg smashed? Was her pretty face ruined?

"Don't worry, Hannah," one of the girls said, arms around me. "She'll be okay. At least she was wearing her seat belt."

Actually, I found out later, Melody was just turning to fasten it, and that saved her from hitting the windshield head-on.

As I watched the paramedics put Melody on a stretcher, I remembered them hauling away Paige not too long before. But my little sister had survived, I told myself. And my big sister would, too. Only she might never be the way she was before this accident.

Keith, after a whiny "What about my car?" offered to ride to the hospital with Melody. Dad and I took the other two who'd been riding with them. The kids in the other car said they'd go back to the party and tell everyone what had happened and then go to the hospital. "Oh, man, what a scene!" the driver said.

Since we had to stop for traffic lights and the ambulance didn't, it got to the hospital ahead of us. They had already wheeled Melody into Emergency when we arrived.

"If Mom's still here," I said to Dad, voice trembling, "we ought to let her know about Melody."

"Oh, Lord," he said. "I guess we'd better." A nurse called Grandma's room and told Mom to come down to Emergency.

A few minutes later she rushed over to us, waiting in the hallway. "Oh, I knew I shouldn't have left Paige at home when she was so upset!" she cried. "How is she? Is it bad?"

"It's not Paige. It's Melody," Dad said, and briefly told Mom what had happened.

"You let her go to that fool party!" she accused Dad. "Why would you allow her to do that?"

"Mom, Mom, calm down," I said. "Dad didn't even know about it." And I thought, *If anyone needs to check on Melody, it's you.* Of course, I wouldn't say such a thing, especially when Mom was near hysteria. I glanced around at Melody's friends, who were standing in a clump, scared speechless for a change. It didn't look as if Keith had been hurt after all. The blood on his shirt must have come from Melody.

A doctor came out. "Your daughter's all right," he said. "There's a cut on her cheek, not deep but a bleeder. And it's near the hairline, so the scar will be minimal. Her leg is broken. But it's a clean fracture. Should heal without a problem."

"Can we see her?" Mom asked.

"They'll be bringing her out as soon as they

get a cast on the leg. She's lucky that it wasn't any worse."

"So not to worry, folks," Keith, the moron, piped up.

Angrily, Mom turned to him. "Don't you tell us not to worry, young man," she said. "I *do* worry about my daughters. You were driving, I assume?"

"Yeah, and my dad will go ballistic when he finds out I wrecked his car."

"I hope he does," Mom retorted. "You should be arrested."

"Calm down, Sharon," Dad said, putting his arm around Mom's shoulder. "As the doctor said, it could have been much worse."

The other girl who'd been in the car said, "At least Melody's face isn't smashed up. That'd be the end."

"Does Grandma know why you left?" I asked Mom.

"No, thank goodness. I just pretended the nurse had signaled from the hall that visiting hours were over. I'll fill her in later." Mom let out an immense sigh. "Here I thought it was Paige, but instead it's Melody. She looked at me. "Don't you be next."

"I won't."

Dad put his arm around me. "This girl is the one we can depend upon. Right, honey?"

"Right, Dad," I said.

Besides the cast on her leg, all Melody had when she came home was a Band-Aid on her cheek. Later, when it was removed, there was the tiniest of scars. "It'll make me look mysterious," Melody said.

As for her broken leg, my sister managed to turn that into a minor melodrama. Lying on the sofa, she talked endlessly to her friends about the fateful night. "We were so close to winning," she told a girl named Marci. "We'd sweet-talked the manager of Taco Bell to let us get behind the counter, even got him to snap the photo, and we'd found a theater showing the right movie. And then we realized we'd used up the film. So I called my sister . . ." and so on. It began sounding, after a while, like a candidate for a TV Movie of the Week.

Melody had a constant stream of visitors, who brought her flowers, chocolates, balloons, and disgusting stuffed animals. Fortunately, Aunt Helen was staying with Grandma, now back at her house, so she missed most of the commotion.

When she did come over, though, she let Mom know what she thought right in front of Melody. "You should exert a little discipline here, Sharon."

"What do you mean?" Mom was foolish enough to ask.

Aunt Helen didn't mince any words. "For starters, you shouldn't have let Melody go to that wild party."

"I . . . I didn't know about it," Mom said.

"Well, you should have."

Melody piped up. "Aunt Helen, don't blame Mom. How was she supposed to know if I didn't tell her?"

"Well, why didn't you?"

Melody smiled. "She might not have let me go."

With a huge sigh, Aunt Helen flung out her hands. "I give up. I'm going back to Phoenix, where life is a dream instead of a nightmare."

Melody rolled her eyes and whispered to me, "That's the best news I've heard all week."

Grandma, who was almost back to normal, rode with us when we took Aunt Helen to the airport.

"Mother," my aunt said, "think about what I suggested, that you move to Phoenix and live with me."

"Yes, indeed, I will," Grandma said. (Later she told us she'd rather eat pins and die.)

At the boarding gate Aunt Helen kissed Mom and Grandma good-bye and then turned to me. "Hannah, you're a wonderful girl. You just try to stay normal in this crazy family of yours"

"Almost all the passengers have gone aboard," Mom told her sister gently. With a final wave Aunt Helen left.

"What a relief," Mom said, as we were driving home. "I love my sister, but I have to say she's a giant pain. How did you put up with her, Mother, all those years you were raising us?"

"You weren't such a pleasure yourself, Sharon," Grandma said with a laugh. "Sometimes I wondered what I'd done to deserve such hellions."

Mom laughed, too. "I guess you're right."

"Do you think, Mom," I asked from the back seat, "that in years to come you'll say the same thing about all of us?"

Mom met my eyes in the rearview mirror. "Hannah, I'll say then what I say now. You're the only one of my daughters who doesn't give me grief. I don't know what I'd do without you."

I turned to look at the scenery outside. I knew now what I'd probably known all along. Although Mom didn't often say so, and in fact seemed to take me for granted, she really did need me. I could never abandon her and go to live with Dad—not on a permanent basis. I'd have to content myself with being with my father whenever I could.

I thought again of the game I'd played with Cheyenne and Kelsey. *Who would Mom save?* In our family, it looked as if I was the one who was actually doing the saving.

sixteen

After a while, things pretty much returned to normal.

Cheyenne took the two kittens, as promised, and Paige was allowed to keep Marmalade in the house part of the time. Butterfly came and went, not too concerned about being almost free of her little family. "She's got the right idea," Mom said. "Love 'em and leave 'em." I don't think she actually meant it, though.

I had, however, noticed a change in Mom's attitude. Maybe some of the things Aunt Helen said had sunk in. For example, we were all watching TV one night, and Melody said, "Hannah, would you go get me some ice cream? Not coffee, I'm tired of it. The chocolate chip."

As I started to get up, Mom said, "Melody,

your sister isn't your servant. Go get your own ice cream." And when Melody put on her injured look, Mom added, "You can get around when you want to, I notice."

Even Paige came in for criticism. Now when she whimpered about not being treated fairly, Mom would say, "Don't give me that, Paige. You're eight years old. Act it. And stop the whining."

As for me, Mom's main complaint was that I spent too much time with Dad and Lauren. "I thought you couldn't stand that son of hers, what's his name? Jesse?"

"He's not so bad anymore," I said. "His mother has really clamped down on him."

"Good for her," Mom said in an approving tone that surprised me. But I'd noticed her disposition had improved since she and Steve made up and were seeing each other again.

She had plenty of time to see him the weekend right after Thanksgiving, because both of my sisters and I were at Dad's. I'd been surprised that Melody had consented to go. It was probably because the novelty of hobbling around on crutches had worn off, so she was no longer the center of attention with her crowd. Or maybe it was because she and Keith had been on the outs ever since the accident.

On Saturday night we were sitting around Dad's kitchen table playing cards when Melody idly asked what we were doing for Christmas.

"I'll bet what you mean," Paige said, "is what is Dad getting you?"

"No, Miss Mouth," Melody said. "I meant what I said. Are we going to be here or at Mom's?" And then she added, "I suppose you have plans with Lauren and her kid."

Dad put down an ace of hearts. "Gotcha!" he said, pulling in the cards he'd just won. "As for the holidays," he said, next playing the queen of hearts, "let's talk about that tomorrow when Lauren stops by."

She drove over the next afternoon, wearing a really cute red cashmere sweater and black skirt. A red velvet headband held back her dark hair, and her nails matched the color perfectly. I could almost hear Melody taking mental notes.

"Sweetheart," Dad said, putting his arm around Lauren, "I haven't told the girls. I thought we should tell them together."

"What?" Paige said the word I was thinking.

And suddenly I knew. "You're getting married!" I burst out.

The two of them looked at each other and laughed. "Is it so obvious?" Dad asked.

"You're getting married?" Melody's mouth dropped open. "Oh, my God!"

And then the three of us were hugging them while babbling away with questions they couldn't answer all at once.

"Okay, okay," Dad said. "Let's pretend this is a presidential news conference. One question at a time. You, Melody."

"Uh . . . when?"

"The day after Christmas," Dad replied.

"Where?" I didn't wait to be asked.

"Here in town, at Lauren's church."

"Big wedding?" I asked out of turn.

"No," Lauren said. "Just family and a few friends."

"Are we invited?" Paige asked, hopping up and down.

"Well, of course." Lauren leaned down. "We want you, Paige, and your sisters to be part of the ceremony."

That finished the so-called news conference. We all began talking. There was more hugging and kissing, too. It seemed that the three of us would be junior bridesmaids. Jesse would also take part. Then the day after that he'd start his Hawaiian trip with his father.

"And what will Mom be?" Paige blurted out.

"Ticked," Melody said under her breath.

"Actually, I think your mother and Steve plan to take you girls somewhere for a few days after the wedding," Dad said. "I don't know where, so don't ask."

"Probably Disneyland," Paige said, hope in her voice.

"What about Grandma?" I asked.

"I don't know for sure, but I assume she'll go along," Dad said.

"So," Melody said in relief, "that whacks the tail off Mickey Mouse and friends."

In all the excitement, no one had asked if Mom knew about the wedding plans. But of course she did.

When Paige gushed out the news—instantly —Mom only smiled and said, "So they told you."

"You knew? And didn't tell us?" Melody asked.

"I thought your father should break the news. I'm happy for him. And for Lauren."

She didn't seem to be faking it. I guess any lingering feelings she'd had for Dad had finally disappeared.

Paige was still caught up in the excitement. "Dad says you and Steve and Grandma and all of us are going on a trip right after the wedding and Christmas. Where?"

"Maybe to a lodge up north," Mom said. "Steve said he'd teach you girls how to ski."

"How wonderful to go through all that. I already have a broken leg," Melody said. "Just kidding."

The early weeks of December seemed to fly. There were school programs, neighborhood parties, friends' parties. And there were the traditional things like decorating the house and shopping for presents and wrapping them. But the biggest excitement of all was, of course, the wedding.

Lauren would be wearing pale, pale green silk with white trim. Melody and Paige and I were to have especially designed dresses of white with green velvet accents. We would all carry nosegays of white roses with long green streamers.

"Thank goodness I got rid of the cast in time," Melody said as we were getting dressed for the ceremony. "Wouldn't it be awful if I were the center of attention?" When we didn't reply, she laughed and added her usual "Kidding!"

Glowing with candlelight and loaded with gorgeous white poinsettias, the church looked beautiful, and I think we all did, too. At least I felt beautiful. I know Lauren did, with her hair done up in soft swirls, laced with tiny white flowers. When I saw her coming down the aisle, I knew what the phrase "stars in her eyes" really meant.

And yet, underneath, I couldn't help feeling a little sad. Our lives were changing, and I knew they'd never be the same. Our family had rearranged itself, with new people. I wondered if Mom and Steve would get married now, too. Well, no use wondering. Why not just ask?

When I got home, I put the question to Mom. She answered by saying, "How would you feel about it?"

This was something new. Since when did my opinion count?

"I think you should go ahead and marry Steve if you love him," I said. "He's already like one of the family." He'd never be like my father, I thought. But that was all right. Steve wasn't the type to try taking over Dad's role.

"Then that settles it," Mom said, with a relieved look. "I was a little worried about your reaction."

"What about Melody and Paige?" I asked.

"Oh . . ." Mom gave a little wave of her hand. "Those girls don't care."

I guessed she was right. My sisters were too wrapped up in themselves.

The night after the wedding, we finally got around to opening presents. Steve was there, and so was Grandma. In future years Lauren and Dad might be with us, if everyone got along all right. And possibly Jesse. It occurred to me for the first time that it might actually be interesting to have a brother, if only a step-brother. In time would he get so mellow I could boss him around? Doubtful.

The next day Grandma and I waited indoors while the others loaded up the van.

"Well, the year's almost over, and what a year it has been," she remarked. "A paramedic parade, first with Paige and then with Melody. Not to mention my stupid stroke, from which I've merci-fully recovered. And then the wedding!" She gave a little smile. "What was that expression you used, about people being loony?"

"Oh, yes. Moonburned," I said. "Too long under the rays of the moon."

"Well, I think our lives have been a little that way this year. All muddled and moonburned."

"You're so right about that," I said.

"But in spite of it all, we've survived."

"So you think everything will be okay from now on?" I asked.

"Oh, honey, things always happen. But it's not so much what happens as how we deal with it. We should take life's changes and say, 'Am I going to let this control me or am I going to handle it?'" Grandma patted my hand. "Now, with you, I have no worries."

"What about the others? Melody and Paige?"

Grandma gave a little laugh. "They'll manage. But they have to learn what it seems you were born knowing. How to cope."

"Maybe it comes from being the middle child."

"Maybe. But I'm inclined to think it's just you, Hannah. You're the way you are. And we couldn't love you more. Any of us. There's only one thing . . ."

"What's that, Grandma?"

"You're there for all of us. Always. But now you need to be there for yourself."

I looked at her, confused.

"Give yourself a break. Appreciate who you are. Because, believe me, Hannah, you're special."

I felt a glow. But all I said was "I'll try, Grandma."

I put my arms around her and she held me close. She didn't say anything else. There was nothing else she needed to say.